BOBBY'S SONG

BOBBY'S SONG
Meeting Again

RICK NICHOLSON

iUniverse, Inc.
Bloomington

Bobby's Song
Meeting Again

Copyright © 2013 by Rick Nicholson

All rights reserved. No part of this book may be used or reproduced by any means, graphic, electronic, or mechanical, including photocopying, recording, taping or by any information storage retrieval system without the written permission of the publisher except in the case of brief quotations embodied in critical articles and reviews.

This is a work of fiction. All of the characters, names, incidents, organizations, and dialogue in this novel are either the products of the author's imagination or are used fictitiously.

iUniverse books may be ordered through booksellers or by contacting:

iUniverse
1663 Liberty Drive
Bloomington, IN 47403
www.iuniverse.com
1-800-Authors (1-800-288-4677)

Because of the dynamic nature of the Internet, any web addresses or links contained in this book may have changed since publication and may no longer be valid. The views expressed in this work are solely those of the author and do not necessarily reflect the views of the publisher, and the publisher hereby disclaims any responsibility for them.

Any people depicted in stock imagery provided by Thinkstock are models, and such images are being used for illustrative purposes only.

Certain stock imagery © Thinkstock.

ISBN: 978-1-4759-6630-5 (sc)
ISBN: 978-1-4759-6632-9 (hc)
ISBN: 978-1-4759-6631-2 (e)

Library of Congress Control Number: 2012924314

Printed in the United States of America

iUniverse rev. date: 01/08/2013

This book is dedicated to the memory of my mother, Vera May Blanchard. As the saying goes; God only gives you 'one' mother, and I'm sure glad he gave me you…Miss you everyday, Love Rick

CONTENTS

1. The Meeting 1
2. Leroy Mingus 16
3. Charlie Butler from the Nam 38
4. The Twins 49
5. My Little Fishing Buddy 61
6. The Orange Man 76
7. Trip to Vegas Part 1. Eddie 92
   Trip to Vegas Part 2. Mary Jane 106
8. Mom sure loved that song 120

ACKNOWLEDGEMENTS

First off I'd like to thank my lovely wife, Christy, for helping me with this book, and everything she does. You've been there with me through the good times and bad and I'm certain you've helped me become a better man. In our 36 years together you have been, my best friend, and lover, but most of all you've been a joy to be with, and I don't know what I'd do without you…I love you with all my heart, Rick

A big thanks to my good friend Sharon Millet, who took my very rough manuscript and cleaned up my jumbled mess of misspelled words, missing quotations and run on sentences. Thank you for helping to make my book easier to read.

Finally, I'd like to thank all my girls; Christy, Danielle and Amie for helping me with the sketches and drawings, including a few groovy ideas along the way, and of course the moral support. Thanks girls, 'Pop Pop.'

INTRODUCTION

The first of these stories came to me in a dream I had about my good buddy, Bob Moore. Bob left this earth suddenly in an auto accident on 1/3/2009. My dream was so cool that I just had to write it down that very morning. In the next few days a story developed in my head, then another after that. As my imagination kicked in and ideas came to me, some very interesting characters evolved. Most all of the characters in the stories are, or were people I've known. The adventures that Bob and I get into, helping the departed are sometimes heart warming, and at other times, full of justice and closure. All through the book, my buddy Bob and I grow to know more about each other, and the other side. Bobby of course, was one of the best pals, I've ever had. As they say; If you can count the good friends you've had on one hand as you go through life, you should consider yourself lucky. See you soon, pal.

I hope you enjoy my stories,
Rick Nicholson

COMMENTS

"Rick has always been a great story teller; now he's put his talent into writing. It's a great way to keep the memory of our friend Bob alive while taking you on their adventures. Rick makes you feel as though you are right there with them on their investigations." You won't be disappointed!

Rickard C. Forsberg, DDS (Dr. Forester)
El Dorado Hills, CA

"A story that anyone who has lost a best friend would enjoy." Rick Nicholson, has created a collection of humorous, and heart warming stories. I felt as though I was there. I am looking forward to more.

Jim Lillpop (Lenny)
Cool, CA

"A series of adventures shared between old friends that keeps the spirit of my Dad's memory alive." If my Dad was here today he would be truly honored to read your book. Thanks, Rick.

Kerstin Petterson (Bob's daughter)
Cool, CA

CHAPTER 1.

The Meeting

I became good friends with Bob, probably from the time we met some twenty years ago at the local watering hole in our little town in the Sierra foothills of northern California. Bob, was sometimes called the "Mayor of the town" because he knew everybody and almost everything about them. He owned a popular automotive repair shop in our part of the county; if he didn't fix your car, he most likely "fixed your neighbor's." As the years went by I discovered he wore many hats and had several careers. He was easy to get to know, and we clicked and became best pals right off. He was, by far, one of the nicest guys you'd ever meet. When you got into a conversation with Bob, over a few frosty adult beverages at the Moonglow Saloon, you most likely walked away having learned something you didn't know and sure as hell could take to the bank. Well not always; sometimes he would bullshit you and take an opposite side just to see if you would fold! That guy was extremely intelligent, funny and humble. But most of all Bob was loyal.

My friend Bob, was also a Marine who served in Vietnam during the late 60's but you never heard him talk about it. I thought Bob was a very good judge of character with most folks he'd meet, which is rare. I would sometimes ask his opinion about a potential customer of mine. The one time that I chose to ignore his advice it bit me right in the ass...damn it!

Because I was a builder for many years with most of my jobs out of town, Bob would sometimes travel with my wife Chrystal, to the job sites to check out my project, maybe have dinner somewhere new and then play golf in a new town. That little guy (Bob was only about 5' 4") was a really skilled golfer; he taught me to play and man we played every chance we got.

We got so close that we started to have annual trips together as well as spur of the moment getaways on occasion. One year Bob, and his "wife" Lorna. I say it like that because he was married a couple of times, and may have been a good judge of character with most folks but had shit poor taste in women. Lorna could be and was a Royal Bitch at times. Anyway, one year they joined us on a trip back east to Baltimore to see my family during the Christmas holidays which was a real fun trip. My folks really loved Bob, especially my step dad, who made Bob put up the Christmas lights on the front of the house. Well, Bob shouldn't have offered!

This story really begins four years after my dear friend Bob, was killed in a car crash on our local highway. The night it happened Bob was delivering a customer's car just about a mile or so from his shop; it was a real foggy night with visibility maybe twenty to twenty five feet and they say my buddy might have been traveling a bit too fast as well. Without going into all the details they say he crossed the double yellow line on the curve by the Grange Hall and smacked head on into a car driven by an older couple.

Bob was killed instantly and the older folks were badly injured but survived the accident. Our daughter, Danielle, coincidentally was in the first car to arrive on the scene after the crash and was able to offer assistance to the older folks as yet another person was already tending to Bob. Danielle never knew it was Bob in the other car until the next day.

The family had a wake and celebration of life a few days after Bob, was cremated and it seemed like the whole town was there. A few of us got up to speak about our friend and tell funny stories which was hard, but I'm glad I did. I remember being in a daze that day with a broken heart like I've only felt one other time in my life; when I lost my Mother just a few months before. A few of Bob's closest friends and I got together and made a memorial at the crash site which was real cool; we put up a cross another friend had made. We dropped some flowers, placed a couple of golf balls on the cross, and left a few pictures.

I used to think those roadside memorials were corny and kinda hokey but I knew I could NOT be left out and just had to be a part of this. Man, I'm glad I was there.

There's a few of us that often stop by Bobs memorial, I know this because something new shows up from time to time. Some folks that loved Bob, would maybe mow down the high grass around the makeshift cross or plant flowers; still others would simply leave a golf ball or picture or something. I think somebody must have gone to Mardi Gras one year because there were a few strands of those cheap ass beads everybody comes back with hanging on the cross along with the golf balls, three or four of which were mine.

Well, as I said earlier it had been about four years since Bob, passed on and as I was driving by one day I had the most undeniable urge to stop. I hadn't stopped in awhile so I pulled over; I didn't have a golf ball or anything to leave but thought, hell, he won't care. I'll just stand there and talk to my old buddy for a spell...

So there I was looking down at the cross telling Bob, how I missed him and how screwed up things seemed to be these days when I heard, "Rick," "say what," I thought, man I haven't even had a drink yet. Am I hearing things? Then again..."Hello, Rick, it's me, Bob." What the fuck!! I thought for sure I was hearing things until I turned around and saw right smack in front of me was my old buddy, standing there smiling. It sure as hell looked like him in jeans and a tee shirt with a ball cap on. Hell, that's all he ever wore unless it was summer; then it was a pair of shorts, tee shirt and a ball cap. Anyway, I thought this was a joke so I reached out to touch him but couldn't. The next thing that occurred to me was that maybe I was dreaming or maybe I got hit by a car while getting out of my truck and was standing there as a spirit myself. In any case, I was freaking out. Bob spoke to me again and told me to calm down and that this was for real; he said he didn't understand it either but said to believe him, it's the real deal.

At this point I thought to myself, if I am dreaming then just go with it because it was cool to see my old buddy Bob. But just then a delivery truck went by and I got not only the breeze from it zooming past but some road grit flew up and hit me in the arm. Then I knew this was the "real deal" as he put it.

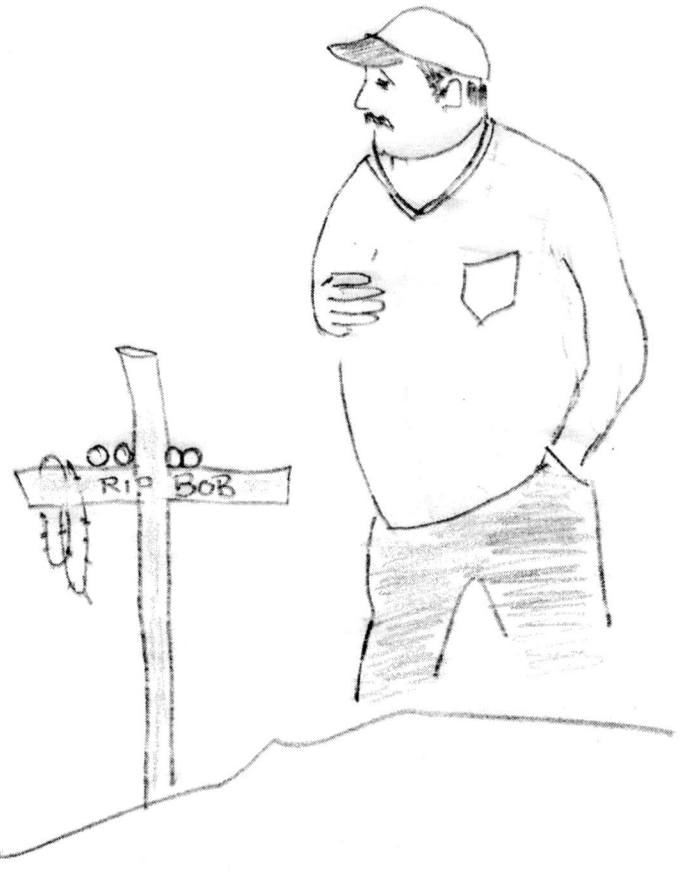

So now here I am talking to Bobs spirit alongside the road and God only knows what people must be thinking, so I said to him "Dude, people are going to think I'm really weird standing here all this time talking to this cross." Bob replied, "don't worry about it, just get into your truck and I'll explain it all to you the best I can."

"Rick," he said, "what I can tell you is while we were outside talking by the cross...hey, by the way, thank you guys for that." Bob went on, "you would think twenty minutes would have gone by but in this cosmic realm or karmic level or whatever you want to call it that I'm in, only moments have passed." "Bob," I said, "do you know you've been gone for nearly four years now?"

"No, Rick, I didn't" Bob replied. "I can't explain it and you know me, that's driving me crazy but it seems like it's only been maybe a couple of weeks in here; wherever here is." "Yeah man," I said, "I can see where that would drive you a little crazy, as anal as you could be, buddy." "So I guess in a way it's a good thing your not here, Rick, so stop worrying about that, it just, is what it is," said Bob.

"Man this is not only weird but kinda cool being able to chew the fat with you again, buddy," I said. "I got a great idea, why don't we head on down to the Moonglow and sit on the back deck and catch up, cause a lot has happened since you passed on." "Sounds great, Rick, let's go," Bob replied.

As we sat there on the back deck of the Moonglow Saloon which was the only bar in our fair little mountain town, we talked about friends, family and people in town. We reminisced about everything from the trips we would go on, like the Drag Races down in southern California, and weekends up the coast for Chrystal's birthday, plus all the golf courses we played on. And, of course, all the years we spent in the Moonglow having fun when Chrystal and I used to own it. Yeah, we owned this joint for a while from '95, until '05 I think. It was a shit poor investment as far as investments go, but man, we had a lot of good times here and made a few lasting friendships, too. And a few I'd like to forget as well. I told Bob how the old gang fell apart right after he died. "Sorry," Bob, replied, "shit like that happens where your at, Rick."

Bob knew the crazy old broad that had it now, as did the whole town. Most people, I think, couldn't wait until something either happened to her and she lost the bar or just simply went away… which ever one came first. She was one of those know it all types that didn't really know shit, you know, like a liberal. She also didn't know shit about what real friendship was or honesty; plus, on top of that she was a sloppy drunk and just about an all around pain in the ass that put her mouth in gear before her brain kicked in.

Nowadays there was a very different kind of crowd that came into the Moonglow that called themselves regulars. Not anything like the good folks that were regulars back in our day, well with the exception of a few 'fair weather' types. Our crowd, was a mixture of blue and white collar folks that played hard and were honest, unlike this crowd that was a mixture of druggie gangster punks and wannabe cowboys. Anyway, it was still the only watering hole in town so you kinda looked passed all that bullshit, had your drink and left.

"Hey Rick, how's business?" Bob asked, "Are you busy?" "Not really, Bob," I replied. "I actually stopped contracting about a year ago and took a course on the internet to try something one hundred and eighty degrees from swinging a hammer. Would you believe I got a license to be a Private Investigator?" "No shit Rick, you a PI, no way," Bob says. "Who do you think you are, Rick, Magnum PI, come on really?"

"Yes, way, and its kinda cool," I said. "It wasn't as hard as you might think; as a matter of fact I did the whole course on the computer. And believe it or not I've just recently been contacted by the Sheriffs department. They called me to come into their office to talk about a drug dealer in the area they think comes in the Moonglow, along with his crowd."

"So, Bob, do you remember old Smoky who lived down the road? And do you remember that piece of shit son of his who was always high on something, that lived with him? They called him Starfish, what a stupid fucking nickname that is, huh? I asked." "Sure I remember him," said Bob, "he was one of the last survivors from the days the Moonglow first opened in the thirty's. And yeah, his son's a piece of shit." "Well, he's the guy they're looking at. I guess he's the new meth dealer in the area and they're thinking he's got a meth lab up there in Smoke's old farm house. They've asked me to keep my ears and eyes open and the State of California's going to be paying for my time. And who knows, this could work into a good gig for me." After a while of reminiscing, we said, goodbye and promised to meet up again soon.

A couple nights later while snooping around Smokes old farm house I noticed that all the windows were covered with aluminum foil and duct tape was covering the cracks. I thought what a bunch of stupid hillbilly fuckers these morons are. Just about the time I was looking for a way in I heard a car coming up the gravel driveway, so I got outta there as quick and quiet as I could and made my way back to my truck down the road. Sitting in my truck I was surprised to see Bob just staring at the moon.

"Hey, Bob, what are you doing here?" "I thought you might need some help, my friend," he said.

Bob pointed to the end of the driveway, and told me that Smoky was standing there. "I don't see anything," I said. He told me that he was very opaque and harder to see even for him because, as he understood it, the better a person you were in life the less visible you were to other Spirits. That meant you were almost done here on earth and closer to the end of life's cycle and closer to heaven; and old Smoky had been a real good man, a loving husband and father and was always there for a friend in need.

Hell, if you knew him you could call him anytime of day or night for a ride home from the bar if you were too drunk to drive or ask him for a ride to the hospital or grocery store or whatever. But it seemed by his presence that old Smoky still had a small item to take care of before he moved on to the end.

Bob went on to explain that he couldn't communicate with him verbally but they could understand each others thoughts and that he could feel the sorrow he saw in his eyes as well, and he knew that Smoky was very sad at how his little boy had turned out. Who wouldn't be, I thought. Bob went on to explain how he's had a word or two with other passing spirits, but he's discovered that he can only really communicate well with other spirits like himself, and of course the darker ones…"you want to avoid the darker ones," said Bob.

Next thing I knew Bob was gone, so I was thinking I'd better leave and come back tomorrow night. To my surprise, a few minutes later Bob was back giving me all the details on what, and who's inside Smoky's farm house. "There's a make shift lab on a picnic table, and just a few boxes here and there; I'm guessing that stupid moron must have sold all of his dads furniture for dope," Bob said. "Shit man, there's nothing there, not even a bed?" I asked. "No, but there are two dirtball dudes and one skanky looking gal in there with him, plus a couple of hand guns by the door.

Make sure you remember that in your report, Rick," said, Bob. "You sure saved me a lot of time buddy, this is just what the Sherriff's department needs to know," I said. "I'll turn this info in tomorrow and let the them take it from there. Thanks, Bob, I'll see you in a couple of days, Okay?" "Yeah, I'll come by your house," Bob replied, "I'll check first to make sure Chrystal's gone so she don't freak out." "Thanks man, that would be good considering I haven't told her about you yet." "No worries, Rick, I'm here just for you right now anyway."

A couple days later the local paper had all the news about the big drug bust and who and what they found. Ha, those morons are going away for a long time. Bob came by and said he was there when the raid went down and saw old Smoky standing there with a tear in his eye and nodding to him as if to say; Thanks, maybe now the boy will get the help he needs. "Well Bob, at least we have one less druggie in town, huh?" I said, "Hey Bob, I was thinking about going away for awhile, I was thinking about going back east to see my sister. Chrystal won't be joining me so I'll be by myself, you want to come with?" "I do," replied, Bob "I'd really like that."

I didn't see Bob on the plane but as soon as I got a rental car, in Baltimore, there he was sitting in the back seat. I told him to get up front so he didn't look like a bitch sitting back there and I didn't have to talk into the rear view mirror; Bob laughed and moved into the front seat.

Our first stop was to my sister Linda's house in Parkville, I didn't tell her I was coming because I didn't want her telling me not to come as I knew she was ill, and that's what she would say. Pulling up to Linda's house Bob asked me if I saw what he saw at the top of the stairs on her front porch. "No, I don't," I said.

"Rick, it's your mother," he said, "waiting there to greet you." I can't tell you the amount of emotions that ran through my body and the chills I felt from head to toe. As I started to cry, I asked Bob, "Why can't I see her?" "I can barely see her myself Rick, but I'm sure it's her, she's very faint but it is your Mom, looking as beautiful as ever. I guess that's why I'm here buddy, so I can see her for you." Bob told me she was looking right at me as we walked up the sidewalk to the front steps. "She's crying, Rick, but all the while smiling and looking right at you with pride." "Can you tell her how much I love her and miss her?" "She knows that, Rick," Bob said. "She told me to tell you that she was there to watch over Linda and would be there with her until the day she passes on. So, to please try not to worry, she'll be with her to guide and comfort her."

As I knocked on the door I could hear my brother in law ask "who's there?" "It's Rick, Gus." "No way," he says. "Yes way, and let me in," I replied. I could hear my sister scream with excitement inside the house.

My sister, Linda, was lying on the couch in her jammies with our Mom now standing right beside her, according to Bob. And wherever my sister went in the house Mom was always by her side or standing behind her. As much as I wanted to see my Mom it just wasn't meant to be; although I tried to squint to see her everywhere in the room. Bob just shook his head and got a chuckle out of that.

"Hey, Rick," Gus asked me, "how long are you here for?" "Only the weekend this time, Pal. I just had to get away for a couple of days because of all the drama I've been going through with my new job. I'm still trying to wrap my head around whether or not I want to do this kind of thing." I thought to myself, as much as I'd like to, I dare not tell them about Bobby hanging out with me, or for that matter anything about Mom. As much as I would love to share my new found gift, that would be one tough deal to explain. Hell, this would have to be a secret that would go to the grave with me.

My sister, and her husband were great. Even with her being as sick as she was, we still stayed up all night and drank the three bottles of wine I brought with me from California. They graciously offered to put me up as I knew they would but considering I showed up unannounced I had went ahead and got a motel room down the road. "I'll see you tomorrow, Hon," I told my sister. "I've got a few old friends to stop and see, that is if they're still alive." "What time will you be here tomorrow, Rick?" Linda asked, "I'll have Gus make crab cakes." "Oooh, crab cakes," said Bob.

"I'll call you tomorrow around noon, goodnight Sis, goodnight Gus." I didn't know where my Mom was in the room and didn't want to look like a fool asking Bobby where she was so I just smiled as I walked to the door and said, "good bye, Mom, I love you," under my breath while covering my mouth, which also made Bob chuckle.

On the way back to the motel I couldn't help but think there was a lot more that Bobby could tell me. "Bob," I said, "do you see people everywhere and are they from both this century and others? I mean, here we are on the east coast where the country was born; do you see people from the seventeen and eighteen hundreds?"

"Rick," replied Bob, "I don't really know yet; just when I think I got it figured out I learn something new. The power of the universe, buddy; I don't think we were meant to fully understand it all. I mean shit man, look at people like the Dali Lama or the Pope; I don't think they knew anything more than me when they pass over unless they have a friend pay them a visit like I did with you. But I will tell you what I do know buddy, and that is there are some people roaming around that are so dark they almost glow with their darkness, if that makes any sense. And I feel sad for some of them and still fear from others. And that tells me that they either lived a lost and sad life or were really "Bad Mother Fuckers" and are better kept at a distance. Plus, I don't think they can even learn anything in this state of their cosmic being or the next, I do occasionally see folks in various shades; from the dark I just described to a faint almost opaque shade like with your Mom and Smoky. People like that seem to be closer to God than the others, Rick, and they aren't meant to be here for long. Kinda like old Smoky; he's gone now you know. Didn't I tell you, I saw him dwindle away and leave us? Have a drink and a cigar, buddy" said Bob, "I'm going to mosey around town a bit, I'll see you in the morning."

As soon as I sat down to breakfast the next morning there was Bob sitting across from me. "How do you do that? I mean how did you know where I would be?" I asked. "I don't know Rick, I just think of you and I'm there wherever you are, weird huh?" "So, where did you go last night, Bob?" I asked. "I went down to the Fells Point area, where you took me that Christmas we came here with you. I went from bar to bar and up and down the streets and let me tell you, there's a lot of lost and wandering spirits here, Rick, and to answer your question from yesterday…"

"Yes! there were men in three corner hats, sailors and ladies dressed in clothes from two hundred years ago, black slaves shackled together, children and immigrants from all over the world. Lots of history here, man, and I found that I can only see a spirit if they want to be seen. If they are really lost and troubled or were a real "bad mother fucker," I know now that they want to be seen, sometimes to the point of annoyance and with a whole lot of anger. I mean, shit, it's hell getting away sometimes. Then there's others who've lived a good life; you know, good people who've died way too soon and innocent children."

"Anyway, I think in that situation they want to see you and you see them so they can share their love again." "Wow, really, that's what you get from some of them?" I asked. "Yeah man, it is. Oh, by the way," said Bob, "I stopped by that Leadbetter's Tavern, you use to work at back in the early seventies. And as soon as I walked in the door they were playing my favorite song, do you remember Rick, I use to play it on the jukebox back at the Moonglow all the time?" I asked, "it was something by Steely Dan wasn't it?" "Yeah, man," replied Bob, "they were my favorite band, remember, it was Reelin in the Years" "Yeah, I remember there were times I could have pulled the plug on that old jukebox too, shit man you played that song every day," I said.

"On the way back to Linda's house I'm going to stop by my Mom's old house on Daniels Avenue. Bob, you don't mind do you?" "Rick, you're really asking me that? I'm just along for the ride, dude." "I was just being funny man, I thought we'd look to see if the Christmas lights were still up." "Just drive the car, Rick," replied Bob.

When we pulled up across the street from Mom's old house Bob immediately told me about a spirit that was sitting on Mom's front porch. As he described him I knew straight away, it was my older brother Tony who had passed away back in '96. He told me how dark and sad of a figure he was and how he was somewhat able to read his thoughts and look into his eyes from across the street. He was waiting for Mom, he didn't know she could only be with one of her children at a time, and she chose to be a guardian to your sister Linda. I think because she needed her the most and that's what Mommas do. "Does that sound about right Rick?" Bob, asked. "Yes it does, my friend, yes it does."

As I sat there and felt for my brother, Tony, who I had a special relationship with and missed very much, I thought about my other siblings and how they treated Tony when he was alive. Some good, but mostly not so good. I thought about how he had made a mess of his life and made some real bad choices from the time he was young man, until he was maybe late forties which always made me sad. He had so much going for himself, but shit happened real early on, like our real father taking off, on Mom and us kids. Hell, I guess that affected all of us in different ways, and it was the drugs and booze that became Tony's crutch. "Hey, Bob, can you communicate something to my brother for me?" I asked. "I can't Rick he's gone already."

"I think he's probably out looking for your Mom, Rick," said Bob. "But I think this will always be a place where you can find him." "That's good to know buddy, lets go back to my sister Linda's to say goodbye," I replied.

Once again Bob, informed me that Mom was on Linda's porch, seemingly waiting for me. Oh, Mom, I thought, I wish I could hold you and give you the biggest hug and kiss. "What was all that about, Rick?" Bob asked. "What do you mean?" I said. "She just gave you the biggest smile and it looks like she's crying a little. Damn Rick, that was heavy; I didn't know that she could read your thoughts, too," said Bob. "That is something I'll have to remember, because when I get back home I'll have to go see my daughter and grandkids again." "Go now, buddy," I said. "Go now, don't worry about me, I'll be fine. But hey, Bob, will I see you again?" I asked. "You will my friend, and remember… 'It's just another day in paradise'."

"You know it is, buddy, you know it is."

CHAPTER 2.

Leroy Mingus

We've been back home now, from our trip to the east coast for about three months. Now that we're back I've got what I like to think is a new and healthier perspective on my life. Truth is, I know now that there's a whole shit load more going on in the universe around us then most folks can even imagine. Only thing is, I'm still not sure whether this new found knowledge is a gift, I've been blessed with or a curse… only time will tell.

Anyway, I used to think that I was just your average guy who grew up in something like an average American family. Ah, maybe not. Hell, my Dad left us so early on that I didn't even know his name. I mean, everybody has a name, right? But considering my older brothers never spoke of him, I just didn't know what to think. That was probably because they hated him for leaving us, and I think too, out of respect for our Mom. By the time I turned thirteen I had almost thought his name was, "Son of a Bitch" and that his nickname was "Ass hole." I did meet up with him when I turned twenty five and sure enough found that those names really did fit him well. Having said that, there's so much more to my family's story, as you can imagine.

I think, my Mom did a hell of a good job raising us. In my eyes she was a Queen; through all the struggle and bullshit she had to endure, she kept us together. And at times did without herself so we had food, clothes and a place to live. Maybe that's what made me what I am today. That and my new found faith in God. After what I just went through, I'll never doubt God again and it makes me very appreciative of every day. As Bob use to say, 'everyday above ground is a good day'. Amen, brother.

It was well into spring now and I was sitting by the river watching the rafters go by, nursing a cold beer and a good cigar. As I turned back from grabbing another Heineken from the cooler, there's Bobby sitting right in front of me as if he's been there all along. "Dude, you got to stop doing that, after what I've been through you're going to scare the shit right outta me!" I said. "What's up and where've you been all this time? I was afraid I'd never see you again, dude."

"Oh, I've been around," he replied, "and like you, I've been reflecting on past events." "Hey, Bob, did you make it over to your daughters house and get to see those grand kids?" I asked. "I did Rick, and they're all doing fine, my daughters doing a real fine job, of raising those little ones. I'm real proud of her and her husband, only wish I could reach out and touch them, ya know?" replies Bob. "I think I do buddy," I answered. "Rick," said Bob, I've been wandering around to all the places I once was while I was alive trying to learn how and why I'm still here, in this place or "dimension." I still don't know what to call it here. But anyway, I wish I knew what it's going to take for me to move on." "Move on to where, Bob?" "To the next level and get closer to the end, I guess," said Bob. "There's not really a Guide or another soul to show me the ropes. Best I can figure is you have to reflect a lot, keep your ears and eyes open to what is and has been, and be humble and remorseful. Then, when you've truly learned your lesson, I think your allowed to move on. It's not rocket science, Rick, but it is something like we've always been taught in Church and the Bible, but with a little "Buddhist" type twist of thoughtfulness sprinkled in here and there."

"You mentioned, 'til you reach the "end," what do you mean by the end?" I asked. "Heaven I guess, or maybe its to be brought back in another body. I'm not sure yet," said Bob. "You mean the reincarnation thing might be for real, Bob?" "I think so, Rick, I really do. Wouldn't it be cool if it is?

So anyway, in my travels I ran across a few old friends from my past and a few from yours, as well." "Hey wait a minute, Bob," I said. "There's no chance I'll come back as a chicken, or a stalk of broccoli is there?" "We'll talk later, Rick," Bob said, with a smile.

"Shall we head up the road to the Moonglow, my friend?" I said. "I'd love to hear all about it." "I Bet I'll beat you there, Rick." "Ha ha, again with the Spirit humor, Bob, you slay me pal. Are all you ghostly dudes assholes, or is it just you?" I asked.

When we got to the Moonglow Saloon I parked my truck and walked inside and was pleasantly greeted by the new owner Lenny Longstreet. Lenny had moved to the area maybe six or seven years ago from Colorado, where his family had been cattle ranchers. They had a big spread down there but I guess, Lenny didn't want that life for himself and his two boys anymore after his folks passed on. Can't say as I blame him either, cold there. One of the things I liked about him was he was a no nonsense, what you see is what you get kind of guy. About 6' 6" and 290 pounds and was just as friendly as can be, but as I said, no nonsense. I worked with Lenny a few times on a couple of remodel jobs and knew that to be a fact. We quickly became good friends.

"Hey, Len, it sure is good to see you standing back there behind the bar instead of you know who," I said. "Thanks, Rick," replied Lenny. "As you know I wanted this place for quite some time, and its going to be hard work to turn it back around after that crazy bitch ran it into the ground, but I'm no stranger to hard work." "I know you're not, buddy, and I also know that this little town is pretty forgiving. Shit, when my wife and I had it we had to turn it around ourselves," I said. "Don't worry it won't take long."

Bobby was once again taking his place, as he did when he was with us, at the end of the bar, pretending to play the video poker machine. "Oh, by the way, heard you had some trouble in here a few nights ago?" I said. "Nothing I couldn't handle, Rick, just another local jerk who can't hold his liquor and got stupid jealous because his wife danced with another guy," said Lenny. "Yeah, I don't miss that shit at all man," I said. "Give me a cold Heineken, will ya Len, and come join me out back for visit, why don't you?" I asked. "I'll join you in a little while, just as soon as this College basketball game is over," replied Lenny. "Cool, see you in a little while, Len."

Bob was already out there on the back deck. We were enjoying each other's company and the view as we had so many times before when Bob started to smile and said, "Rick, can you see that shadowy figure coming towards the bar on a horse, on that hill behind Dr. Forester's office?" "Yeah, I do, what do you think, some lost cowboy?" "Well, my friend, if I'm not mistaken that's old Leroy Mingus. Do you remember him?" "I do, Bob, didn't he use to have that big ranch down the road near the south fork of the river?" I asked. "He sure did, Rick, it's probably the biggest family owned ranch left in northern California. I think it's been in his family since the 1800's. I wonder what he's doing here?" "Well," I said, "he's sure not coming from the dentist office. If I remember right Mr. Mingus only had a half a dozen teeth in his head." "Dude," said Bob, "last time I heard, Dr. Forester had a strict rule against working on dead folks, old Leroy's passed on, what, ten years now?" "Oh yeah, that's right," I replied.

"Howdy boys, how ya'll doing on this fine day?" says Mr. Mingus, as he ever so slowly gets off his horse, then gives her a gentle pat on the rump. As the chestnut mare vanished into the field behind the bar, old Mingus came up the back stairs. I'm surprised that I can see him as clearly as I see Bob. He shakes Bob's hand and gave me a howdy type of nod as he took off his well worn Stetson felt hat, rolled it up and tucked it in his back pocket. "I've been looking for you boys," he says. "Really," Bob replies, "why's that Leroy?" "Yeah, Mr. Mingus how did you know about us anyway?" I asked. "Well, first off, Rick call me Laroy," he says. I whispered to Bob, "did he just say, Laroy not Leroy?" "Yeah, he did," said Bob. "But don't worry about it, that's the way it sounds when he's got a big mouth full of chew. Just call him anything you want, cause he can't hear too good anyway." "Can you get chew on the other side?" I ask Bob. "Of course not, he's just got a great imagination, Rick," Bob replied.

"Boys, did I ever tell you about the time I shot a mountain lion across the street from the bar, right through the front door?" "No, Mr. Mingus, I don't think you did, (fact was I heard the story many times) how'd you do it Leroy?" I asked. "Well, it was maybe 1960 or '61, I think, when somebody came in and said there was a big cat in the field across the street.

So, I said to Irma Wilson, the owner at the time, boy howdy that gal sure was a looker… anyway, I asked Irma if she wouldn't mind if I shot it. She said, okay as long as there was no traffic coming. So I went to my truck parked out back, got my rifle, came back in, propped open the door, sat on a barstool in the doorway and as that cat was peeking it's head over that big rock on the other side of the road I took my shot. Went over and retrieved him after sundown." "That's a hell of a story Mr. Mingus," I said. "Laroy, young fella, please call me Laroy."

"So boys," says old Mingus, "the word is you've been helping folks like me with their troubles and that's what I'm here to talk to you about." Bob asked, "How did you know about that, Leroy?" "Well, Bob, just like breathing, walking and talking folks, spirits like me talk to one and other, too. They complain about their situation, cry and laugh. And then, there's some that are still so full of bullshit, and carry tales just like they did when they was alive and kicking, you'd think they would have learned that lesson in life. Damn fools." says Mingus.

"But I don't care much about that, I only want to make things right with my boys and their families. You boys know my two sons, Earl and Jimmy? And did you young fellas know my lovely wife, Lorraine?" asked Mingus. "Not really, sir, only seen her around town a few times," I replied. "Bob, you knew her didn't you?" asked Leroy. "Sure you did, you worked on her car a few times, didn't you?"

"Fact is I worked on that old Buick more than a few times, but it was just your basic maintenance kind of stuff. That's one beautiful piece of Detroit iron, that Buick," Bob went on to say. "Oh yeah," I said, "I absolutely love that car. I'd be proud to own that ride hell, I'd live in it if that's all I had left to my name and never sell it. That's the kind of car you'd want to enter into a car show, wouldn't you Bob?" I asked. "Not to many '57 Buick Road Masters around anymore." "Yes sir," said Leroy, "my Lorraine sure loved that old riverboat too, Rick."

"You know, boys," said Mingus, "after my Lorraine passed on back in the late 80's, I just didn't want to live anymore. I pert near tried to kill myself a couple times, only thing that keep me from doing it was the good book. You know, it says it's a sin and you'll go to hell. And you know boys, that just won't do, because you see, I need to be with my Lorraine again if I can, cause you know as sure as the sun's gonna come up tomorrow my gal's going to be in heaven. And that's where I want to be, right along side of her. She was a special lady, my gal was. Worked the ranch with me close to forty years, was my best friend and lover, and boy could that gal cook and bake too. You know, in all the years we was together she never asked me for anything new, she was just happy to be alive, and was content with things as they were. She knew how to make things last too just like that Buick I bought for her brand new back in '57. She'd wear a dress 'til it was so worn out and the color faded away, then she'd make rags or something out of the fabric. Hell, she just couldn't throw anything away," Mr. Mingus explained, to Bob and I through his tears.

"When I died and got here on this side the first thing I did was to look for my Lorraine, and I found her too. Only thing is I'll never be able to hold her again, I can see her and she can see me, but she's so faded it's like a polaroid picture left out in the sun, the image has started to fade. And what I've learned, boys, is my Gal is not really in the same place as me, she's a lot closer to the end then I'll ever be. My biggest regret is that I didn't live a better life. You know, all those late nights drinking and gambling trips. I sure wish I could take all of that back, and the stuff I did in the war I'm not too proud of neither. But, that was war, and I'm pretty sure God was on our side in that one."

"Yep, had I been a better man maybe I'd be holding my Lorraine right now and who knows, maybe we'd be walking through those pearly gates together. Well, the past is the past, ain't nothing I can do about that now. Having said that, my friends, I still have the chance to make things right with my two boys, Earl and Jimmy if I can, and Lorraine might once again be proud of me."

"Mr. Mingus," I said, "could you please hold that thought, I just gotta get another beer and go to my truck for a cigar. You guys want a beer? Oh, that's right, you…" "Hey, Rick," says Bob, "really, dude? Really? Go get your freaking cigar." "What's the matter you spirits got no sense of humor?" I replied.

By the time I got back to the deck it had only been maybe five or ten minutes. Lenny had a few customers he was tending to so we didn't really chat but a minute or so.

First thing I noticed, Mr. Mingus was not there, but Bob was. "Hey Bob," I said, "where did Mr. Mingus go?" "While you were gone Leroy and I went over to the Mingus Ranch down the road and he showed me around a bit. He showed me the family graveyard, and his wife's headstone he had made special for her, it was beautiful, I gotta say. He had her picture put on it, what a lovely lady she was. Then he took me way back on the property to the mine shaft where the gold was hidden." "Gold, what gold are you talking about? Are you telling me that old man Mingus had gold on his land?" I asked, "And you did all that while I was gone to get a beer?" "Yeah, I sure did, dude. Don't you remember the time warp thing I explained to you awhile back?" Bob said, "and yeah, he's got gold, too and a lot of it."

"Leroy, told me this story while we were on the ranch. He told me about his grandfather coming out west in the 1800's and buying up all that property. He wanted to build a first class cattle ranch and raise a family. Leroy, had always heard his grandpa did a little gold mining somewhere on that piece of land, at least that's the story his dad had always told him. He'd always say, that's how his Pap was able to buy the two thousand acres around him, that later became the Mingus Ranch, with the gold that he had found on that land. Anyhow, as the story goes his grandpa's mine filled up with water, like so many did in those days, so he gave up on it and concentrated on ranching. And ranching is all Leroy's dad ever knew. He was quite good at it, and happy with it, just like his dad, 'Grandpa Mingus' was."

Bob went on to say, "One day, as a young man growing up on the ranch, Leroy happened to stumble upon the mine entrance while out on horse back checking fence. He saw that it was indeed flooded and thought to himself he could get that water out of there with one of the ranch irrigation pumps. But then the war came along and changed everything. The gold mine would have to wait. By the time he got back home at the wars end, he had to keep the mine on the back burner as the ranch needed his attention in a bad way. His folks were getting on in years and the work of keeping the ranch up to par with all the critters, and fields to tend to was just too much for them. So as any good son would do, he worked his tail off day and night to bring the ranch back around to its glory days, which he did. He told me that he and his father never spoke of the gold mine, most likely due to the dementia that his dad suffered from, although he often wondered if he ever knew about it at all?

When his folks passed on, Leroy buried them in the small family cemetery that was just on the rise to the rear of the ranch house. They were laid to rest along side of Grandpa and Grandma Mingus, as was the custom of most ranching families. It wasn't until after, that Leroy married his high school sweetheart Lorraine and started in on raising his own family. The idea of opening up that old mine got pushed back yet again. After the first couple of years together Lorraine gave Leroy two sons. Now there was Lorraine, the ranch, and those boys to take care of."

"The ranch did very well for him and Lorraine, so well that he was able to pay off the small note his Dad had taken out during the war years. In the late 60's he was finally able to reopen that mine. Like most old boys from his generation he worked at it little by little and never gave up on it. He was able to get the water out right away and just as soon as he did he started to find Gold, pretty good size nuggets, and a lot of it too, he said. Leroy, would work the walls of the mine, then would put the nuggets he found in a sock. As the years went by he had filled maybe one hundred or more socks, which he would then put into pillow cases he could stack against the wall. He went on to tell me he had a hard time explaining all the missing socks to his wife and a harder time still, explaining all the missing pillow cases. He said he went to the Sears store quite lot, in those days!"

"I don't get it, Bob," I said, "just what does he want us to do for him?" "Well buddy, what he wants our help with is to help his boys find the mine and that gold. I guess his sons have had a hard time trying to hold onto to the ranch these past few years since the economy took a dump." "Yeah, I hear that," I said, "it's been tough for most people, myself included. Just how are we going to lead his boys to that gold? I don't even know them." "I do," said Bob, "I've worked on all their cars and their kids vehicles, plus all the ranch equipment for years. Now that Scotty has the shop he works on their stuff. So yeah, I know them pretty well. Not to worry we'll figure something out." "You should be proud of that young fella, Bob, Scotty's doing a pretty good job running your old shop, he seemed to take up right where you left off," I said. "He's a real stand up guy, and everyone in town loves him," I added. "Yeah, he's a good mechanic alright, and I am proud of that kid," replies Bob.

I said goodnight to Bob, and headed home to think about this one. I called Chrystal, and asked her if she needed me to pick up anything from the store on my way home, she told me to pick up a nice bottle of wine, to have with dinner. That sounded good.

During dinner, the Anderson Cooper show was on TV and his guest was this lady psychic who I've never seen before. She was spot on with the audience and had folks in tears with the knowledge she had about their deceased family members. I got to thinking that if my private eye career doesn't work out for some reason, maybe I could convince Bobby to partner up with me in the psychic business. I mean, how hard could it be? I'm already talking to dead people whether I want too or not! I can see it now, "The Bob & Rick Show," only on the "E" channel, hmmm… I got to remember to ask Bob how they do it. Then it hit me, I've got to find a psychic who will work with us.

I soon discovered that finding an honest to God real psychic was not going to be as easy as opening the phone book or checking the internet. I asked Bobby if he and Leroy could do their own investigation to help me and hopefully weed out the phonies.

It didn't take long until Bobby and Leroy found out about a gal through that spirit "hot line" Leroy told us about last week. Her name was Stella Morgan, and she lives in Sparks, Nevada. The interesting part here that I never expected is that she already knows what's needed of her and will be calling me to get together and work out all the details.

I guess Mr. Mingus did quite a bit of gambling in the Reno/Sparks area in his day, so for him to be able to travel there was a piece of cake, hell it was just a three hour drive for me. Leroy paid Stella a visit first and told her the whole story. She agreed to help, and did not want any kind of payment, so Leroy told her he'd make sure a tidy sum got donated to her favorite charity instead, which made her very happy.

When I drove up to Sparks, I wondered where Bob was and as quick as that, he was sitting next to me in the truck. "Hi, Rick," he says. "Hey buddy, where you been?" I asked. "Oh, here and there you know." As we got into the Reno area Bob informed me that he wouldn't be joining me at Stella's house but Mr. Mingus would be there. As I'm on the highway doing about seventy Bob says, "Rick, I'm going to get out here and go visit an old golfing buddy. I'll see you later and you can fill me in then." "Sure, do you want me to pull over and let you out?" Bob just smiled and shook his head and was gone. Well, I thought it was funny, and I'll bet he did, too.

As I pulled onto the street to Stella's house I had a preconceived notion of what she might look like, which was a little old Mediterranean type lady with a scarf wrapped around her head and a shit load of beads around her neck. Boy, was I ever wrong. She lived in a real nice part of town in a gated community full of nice condos. When she answered the door I was pleasantly surprised to see a very attractive middle aged women, with shoulder length gray hair and a very pretty face. She kind of reminded me of June Clever, you know, the Beaver's Mom, only shorter. "Hello, I'm Stella," she said in a very soft voice as she stepped out on the porch. "You must be Rick."

"Hello Stella, it's really a pleasure to meet you," I said as I shook her hand. I couldn't help but notice how soft and warm her hands were, and how it actually made me feel at ease and comfortable with her right off. Well, that and her eyes, her eyes were such a deep violet color, they reminded me of a young Elizabeth Taylor. So intense and beautiful you couldn't help but to stare. I apologized for staring, and she said, "No worries sweetie, I get that all the time." I bet you do, I thought to myself. As we walk towards the door she turned to me and said, "I do, really." Damn, can she read my thoughts?

After some small talk and a nice pot of tea and biscuits we shared ideas on how to solve Leroy's problem. I asked her if she had ever channeled anyone to the point where she could write a letter in their handwriting. She said, yes, so I asked her to call on Mr. Mingus so he could dictate a will addressed to his boys. "Good idea," she said.

I excused myself and stepped out onto the back patio for a smoke. Stella said she didn't mind a bit, and that her husband had the cigar habit, too, she made him smoke outside as well. Stella joined me after a while with a couple of cold beers and told me about her first meeting with Leroy. She said she thought he was very lonely and sad and wondered if there might be something she could do to reunite Lorraine and him. I asked, "Can you do that?" "I don't know if I can or not but maybe, just maybe, this gesture will be enough to move him up, closer to her," Stella replies.

"Move him up, you mean there may be a chance he and Lorraine could be together again?" I asked. "I pray that there is, Rick. Let's go back inside now, if you don't mind, I'll be calling on Leroy soon and I never do these type of things outside, the neighbors you know."

We sat at the dining room table and I asked Stella if she was going to light a few candles and if we had to hold hands and chant something. She told me that Leroy had already warned her about my "spirit" humor and that she thought it was cute, and smiled. Just that quick Mr. Mingus was also sitting at the table. I told him he just missed breakfast and they both looked at me at the same time and frowned, then they looked at each other and smiled, shaking their heads. "Hey, I got to have my fun whenever I can," I said.

I asked Stella if she had any real old writing paper. She replied no, so I told her not to worry, and to show me what she had. "Okay" I said, as I held the writing paper she handed me, "we'll just have to make this look old." Leroy lifted his eyebrows and asked, "How do you do that, Rick?"

"Well, Leroy, first I'll take it outside and rub both sides on a dirty car then we'll run it through the quick wash cycle in the dish washer, then iron it lightly, and that should do it."

Leroy said, "Rick, you better make a couple of them just in case." "Okay," I said, "I'll make three will that be enough?" "Should be," he replied. After I dried the papers in the oven and ironed them a little they were ready to use. "Alright, Stella, its time for you to do your magic now," I said. "Alright Rick, it's about damn time and it's not magic, but I guess if you had to call it something it would be closer to Voodoo," Stella replies, "now where'd that chicken run off to anyhow?" "You're kidding, right?" I said. Stella and Leroy just laughed as she pointed her finger at me and said, "gotcha!"

Seated at Stella's dining room table and looking around I can't help but feel very comfortable and at ease in her home. Everywhere I look seems to be taken from a page right out of a Sunset magazine. I was about to ask Stella about the new car in her garage, that I had seen when I went out to the refrigerator to get another beer, when she lifted her finger to her lips like a school teacher shushing me to be quiet.

She then winked and gave me a little smile. Leroy, stood directly behind her with his hands seemingly on her shoulders. As she began to write on the distressed paper we made earlier. I thought to myself, she makes this look easy. After only a few moments she lifted her head and asked me if I would please go to the kitchen and put the kettle on so she could have some tea. "Of course, I'd be happy to," I replied. By the time I got back to the table Leroy was gone and Stella was folding the papers and stuffing them into an old Prince Albert tobacco can, that had been on display in a cabinet in her hallway. That cabinet and others like it around the house were full of old western style knick knacks, belt buckles, old bullets, arrowheads and stuff like that.

I knew that miners used to keep their mining claims, deeds and any kind of important papers stashed away for safe keeping in those tins.

You can sometimes find them out in the desert or up in the hills and sometimes even in antique shops, so I thought how appropriate and clever of Stella to do that. "All that's left to do now, Rick, is for me to contact the Mingus boys," said Stella. "I'll let you know after I do if you'd like." "Yes, please, if you wouldn't mind. I'd love to know how it all worked out," I said.

During the ride back home from Sparks I couldn't help but wonder if Mr. Mingus would ever be with his gal again and I was glad there was going to be a happy ending to this story.

I also couldn't help but to wonder, just how much gold was in those pillow cases anyway? Oh, well, those boys of his are a couple of fine young men and their families are nice too, they deserve it. And where was Bobby? I hope we meet up at the Moonglow later.

About a month had gone by now since I met Stella and I'm sitting here in the Moonglow watching a ballgame with Lenny when the phone rings. Lenny passes the phone to me and says it's some lady. "Hello," I said. "Hello, Rick it's Stella Morgan, how are you?" "Oh, hi, Stella, I'm fine thanks, how are you, dear?" I replied. "Well, Rick, I just wanted to give you an update on Leroy Mingus and his boys, Earl and Jimmy," she replied. "Do you have a few minutes?" "Of course," I said, as I grabbed my coffee and stepped outside to sit on the deck.

Stella said, "I called them a few days after you left and asked them if I could meet with them at their ranch, I told them I knew their father and that he had given me a message to give them. They were, as most people would be, a bit apprehensive but agreed to meet with me and gave me directions. Of course, I already knew how to get there. Leroy had given me a complete description of the entire property, plus all the out buildings, including where the opening to the mine was."

"It wasn't to much of a stretch for them to accept the fact that I indeed did know their father, after all he was a gambler and made numerous trips to the Reno/Sparks area to gamble, Stella continued to explain. The hard part was convincing them how I knew their father, and that I wasn't some floozy from Nevada who may have had an affair with him or wanted something. You know, Rick, when Leroy and I wrote his last will and testament he also had me draw a map for his boys so they could find the mine."

"I was happy that his family were open and perceptive to who I was and to what I had to tell them. I guess I can thank psychic's like Jonathan Edwards and others who we've all seen on TV for that. I asked the boys and their wives if they wouldn't mind if we walked around the ranch as we talked since it was such a nice day. As we got closer to the old equipment barn I asked if I could go inside and they told me I was welcome to go anywhere I'd like. Inside the barn was where they kept their Mom's old Buick, you know? I told them that I was drawn to it and asked if they wouldn't mind if I checked it out. No, not at all, please help yourself, the oldest son Earl told me. So I went over to it, I told them, how I thought their Mom's Buick was such a classic and beautiful car, which it is.

Earl, then asked me, how I knew that the Buick belonged to their mother. I told them your father told me so. The car had an old blue tarp covering the back end and the boys kindly removed it so I could get a better look. You know that car must have had a half an inch of dirt on it, Rick. I walked around the old car, took a tissue out of my bag and wiped off the passenger side window and looked inside. So I could get a better look I opened the door and leaned in, then I got into the drivers seat.

I told them that their mother must have felt like a movie star driving this. Then, I reached into the glove box and placed the Prince Albert tin inside, then lifted it right back out." "But how were you able to slip that in there without any of them seeing you?" I, asked. "Piece of cake Rick," she says, "I used to date a magician from Reno many years ago and we played our share of button, button where's the button, if you know what I mean. Plus I helped him practice his act a lot, so I guess you could say, I picked up a few things." "Nice," I said.

"So anyway, Rick, I handed the tin to Earl and told him, "this is for you, your father wanted you to have this." As the family was examining the tin I made my way back up to the driveway and opened the gate so I could drive out. While walking back to my car Leroy's youngest boy Jimmy ran up to me and gave me the biggest hug and softly said in my ear, "Ms. Stella, you knew what was in that glove box, didn't you?" All I could do was smile. "Rick, as I drove off that boy just stood there at the gate watching me, till I was out of sight."

"Stella," I said, "you truly are an angel, you really are." "Not yet, my dear, not quite yet, but hey, I have a feeling you'll be hearing from those Mingus boys real soon." "Well my friend, you know where I live so please, don't be a stranger." And with that she hung up. I thought to myself, man, that was some phone call. Damn my coffee got cold too!

About another month went by, and just as Stella predicted I got a phone call from Earl Mingus. Earl introduced himself to me and asked me if I knew his father, I told him yes but not real well. He asked me if I wouldn't mind meeting him somewhere and that he needed to talk to me about his dad. I of course agreed, and asked him to meet me at the Moonglow Saloon in town. I hoped Bobby would be there.

I got to the Moonglow about thirty minutes after Lenny opened for the day as that was always a real quiet time to meet a client. Bobby was there sitting at the video poker machine as always, no sooner than I lifted my hand to gesture to Lenny for a cup of coffee, the juke box started to play, Steely Dan's Reelin in the Years. I look over to Bob, he looks at me and grins and says, "Cool huh?"

As Lenny hands me my coffee, he mentions how that song plays a lot these days. All I could do was smile, "Is that right?" I said. I took my coffee and waited out back for Earl to show. I didn't have to wait long.

Good manners, I thought right on time. "Hello," he said, "you must be Rick Nelson." "Yes, I am and you're Earl, Leroy's son. I saw your son play football one cold, miserable, rainy day when he was a senior in high school," I said. "No way," says Earl, "there were only a handful of loyal students in the stands, plus my dad and a bunch of his buddies from the bar, you were one of those guys?"

"Yeah, a bunch of us from this bar right here went down there with him. He really loved to watch your boy play football, and was real proud of you, too" I said. "Thanks, Mr. Nelson, well, you must have made a big impression on my dad, and boy, have I got a story to tell you."

He went on to give me a run down of the ranch and it's history, including all that's happened since his dad passed on. I told him that I had really liked his dad, but I didn't know that I ever made that much of an impression on him. "I hardly knew him, as I said, but you know what I just remembered? Your dad and I shared a love for pickled eggs with our beer." Of course if he only knew I'd had a visit from his dad not too long ago.

"I was at your dads wake, at the ranch that day, but didn't stay long enough to meet you and the family because of the crowd," I said. "Yeah, dad sure knew a lot of people." "I'll say," I replied, "I think most of the county was there. Hell, I had to park half a mile down the highway! So, what can I do for you young man?" I asked. "Well, as I said, Mr. Nelson." "Please, call me Rick," I said. "Okay, thanks, Rick, as I was saying, we were just about to throw in the towel, with the Ranch, when out of the blue we got a phone call from a psychic from up in the Reno/Sparks area who said she knew our Dad. We agreed to meet this lady 'cause we all thought, what the hell, why not, and I'm sure glad we did."

"To make a long story short, Rick, this lovely lady showed up at the ranch and after some small talk told us some stuff about Mom and Dad that only family knew, which got our attention. Then she asked us all to go for a walk around the ranch. Once again my brother and our wives looked at each other and said, why not. Rick, when we got to one of the barns she went right over to mom's old dirty '57 Buick and climbed inside. This sweet lady, found dads last will and testament in the glove box in a freaking tobacco tin!" said Earl. "Rick, I've been in that car a dozen times since Dad passed on and I can't figure it out, but I don't really give 'two hoots' about that now, Rick" he said. "There was a map along with that will and that map led right to, are you ready for this… a gold mine."

"Yeah, Rick, my dad had one hell of a hobby," he said. "So, Earl, was there any gold in the there?" I asked. "Like you wouldn't believe, Rick. There's such a massive amount they're saying that its turning out to be the largest gold discovery in California since the 1800's." "No shit," I said, "how large we talking about?"

"Well, Rick, my dad had over one hundred old pillow cases full of socks that were each full of gold nuggets. Each pillow case weighed between two and three hundred pounds." "WTF? Are your shitting me?" I said, as I about choked on my coffee. "No, I'm not shitting you, Rick." Earl continued. "And there's still a vein on each side of the mine shaft that could go on for a half mile, say the engineers." "Holy mother of God," I replied. "They're saying the conservative estimate on just the pillow cases that dad filled, is sitting right now at approximately 800 million dollars," said Earl. "Holy Mother of God" I said, again! "I guess you don't have to be Ranchers anymore huh?"

"My God, I've never been this fucking blown away in my life," I said. "I want you to hold that thought for a little while, Rick. Let me buy you a beer." "Sure," I said. "Hey Lenny, you're not going to believe the story I have to tell you man," I said. Earl asked Lenny for a draft beer and tells him to give me whatever I want and lays down a credit card. "You know, Rick," says Earl, "my dad also left a request in his will that the family make a donation to a homeless shelter up in Reno, Nevada, which we were more than happy to do. Rick, there's so much money that's come from dad's gold that one hundred people couldn't spend it in as many lifetimes, so the family decided to give a large donation to every homeless shelter in the United States." "Wow, that's the nicest thing I've ever heard," I said. "Well," replies Earl, "thanks to my dad, maybe some folks can get a fresh start and not have to sleep outside for awhile." Just then, I happened to look over my shoulder and see Bob standing with Leroy, both of them grinning from ear to ear.

"My dad had one more request in his will, Rick, which is mainly why I'm here. Can you step outside with me for a moment?" asked Earl. "Sure, of course I can," I said. As I step outside and turn my head, WTH! I couldn't believe my eyes, there sitting at the end of the parking lot was what looked to be Lorraine Mingus's '57 Buick Road Master. Only this car looked "Car show" quality, better than any I've ever seen. "Wow," I said, "is that your mom's old Buick, Earl?" "No, Rick," he replies, "that's your new Buick." "What? What do you mean, my Buick?" I asked. Just then, Earl's brother, Jimmy Mingus walked up and handed me the keys and said, "Here you go, Mr. Nelson." "Our dad," said Jimmy, "wrote in his will that he wanted you to have mom's car." Earl added, "we talked about it and decided that we couldn't just wash it and give it to you the way it was, so we sent it to a custom car shop down in southern California. You might have heard of it, Chip Fosse Customs?" "Yeah, I've heard of him alright," I said. Jimmy adds, "There's not another one like it in the world

Mr. Nelson. They did a complete restoration with all new drive train and state of the art components. Of course all new interior and, how do you like the leather upholstery with your name embossed in the headrest." "Yes, it's beautiful," I said, "but…"

"Mr. Nelson," says Jimmy, "it rides nicer than a brand new Cadillac with a 502 big block and about 600 horse power. We hope you like it." "I do, I'm just so fucking blown away, thank you boys, thank you very much," I said. "We don't know why or what you did for our dad, Mr. Nelson, and I'm quite sure it was more than sharing a love for pickled eggs, but whatever it was, thank you, from the Mingus family," said Earl.

As Leroy's boys drove off I waved goodbye and that's when I saw old Leroy sitting on his horse across the road waving back at me. Leroy, took his hat off and says, "Thank you, my friend," and simply rode away, until he vanished…I thought, to myself, I sure hope he gets to be with his gal Lorraine again one day.

CHAPTER 3.

Charlie Butler from the Nam

It had been a while since we'd (Bobby and I) said goodbye to Mr. Mingus and his boys. I was staying fairly busy with a few jobs for the State and a couple more in the next county. I took out a small ad in the neighboring county's local paper because I didn't really want people in my town knowing what I was doing for a living now. As far as they knew I was just a retired contractor that's all they needed to know anyway.

The state of California has a set scale as to what they pay and it's fair enough, I guess, but it takes thirty days or more to get your damn money. Hell, that was the same deal with most larger jobs I did back when I was a contractor so that's okay. Between that and Chrystal's job we get by pretty good.

So now here we are, Bob and me, just like the old days sitting in the Moonglow Saloon. I'm talking to the new owner, Lenny Longstreet when out of nowhere the jukebox starts to play that damn Steely Dan song again. I look over at Bob sitting in front of the video poker machine and ask, "Hey, dude, how did you do that?" Bobby just looks at me with a shit eating grin and says, "I got it down now buddy."

"Hey, Len," I said, "let me have an ice cool Heineken, will ya." "Sure thing Rick," he says. "So, Len, I gotta tell you," I said, "it sure is great you getting the bar and keeping it open, everything going well?"… "Rick, life is good," replies Lenny. "I'm making my bills and even making a little profit. That along with meeting some great people and playing music on my own stage I'm thinking, can it get any better than this?" "It can always get better pal, but I'm glad to hear it."

While chewing the fat with Lenny I caught Bobby out of the corner of my eye stand up and gaze out the window like he was a little kid and the newest Chevy was coming down the road. "Hey, Bob, what's up?" I asked, "Do you see something?" "Yeah man, I think I see someone I used to know but I'm not sure," he says. "I don't see anybody," I replied. "You won't, Rick, he's like me. I'll be right back."

I took my beer and went to sit on the back deck, so I could smoke a cigar, and look out at the hills behind the firehouse, for a spell. After a while Bobby came back with a friend, and to my surprise I could see his friend as clearly as I could see Bob. "Whoa, this is getting weird, Bob, how can I see your friend?" "Because he wants you to see him, Rick," Bob answered.

"Rick, I want you to meet my friend Charlie Butler," said Bob, as he put his arm on Charlie's shoulder. Charlie, was dressed in old military fatigues that were pretty battered and worn and what looked like could have been a few blood stains on the front. "Hi, Rick, how you doing," he said. "Hello, Charlie," I said. "Man I can almost smell your cigar," Charlie replies. "It looks like a good one." "It is," I reply "it's Dominican, I buy them online." "Good idea, Rick," Charlie, whispers to Bob, "where's on line?" "I'll tell you later," Bob, tells him.

"Rick, I knew Charlie from Vietnam," says Bob. "I kind of thought so Bob." "The fatigues huh?" said Charlie. "Well, yeah, that was "forgive the pun," a dead give away," I said. "That and the fact that you're a Spirit like Bob."

"Charlie and I got there about the same time in '68," Bob goes on to explain. "After we were put into the same squad we realized we both came from the Sacramento, area and knew a lot of the same people. Plus we had a lot more in common so naturally, we became friends. Rick, my friend Charlie here was killed one day while we were on a mission, about three months into our tour of duty. He was shot by a sniper who we were able to shoot out of the tree moments later but unfortunately, Charlie was killed instantly." "Forgive me for asking, Charlie," I said, "but what the hell are you doing way up here in the foothills so far from Sacramento?"

~

"Wow," Charlie says, "this place has some good tunes on the juke box." "Yeah, Lenny's about the same age as us and really likes the 50's, 60's and early 70's music so that's all he plays. Nice huh?" I reply. "I always know when I come in and "Alice's Restaurant" is playing he's either gone for a sandwich or he's in the bathroom. Once I even caught him coming out of the office zipping up his pants with a female friend close behind. The damn song is over twenty minutes, plenty of time for some hanky panky."

"Well, Rick, I was looking for my old friend Bob Moore who I knew from the Nam." "Really?" I asked. "Yeah," says Charlie, "I remembered he once told me that he had a girlfriend way up here in this area and, man, I can't tell you what a blessing it was to see him come out of this bar. I've been searching for him for such a long time now." "Why have you been looking for me, Charlie?" asked Bob.

"Well, Bob, do you remember I told you I was married and that my wife was pregnant?" "I do," replied Bob. "Well, my wife, Carrie," says Charlie, "had a son who she named Charlie, pretty original huh? Anyway, he grew up to be a fine young man who later married his high school sweetheart. Later on my little Charlie and his gal had a little girl they named Bunny, it was a picture perfect family until my little Charlie was killed while street racing. All this time I've been watching my family go through their ups and downs and not being able to ever reach out and touch them. Tears your heart out everyday, don't it Bob?" "Yes, it does Charlie," Bob replied. "If they only knew that all they have do is really want to see their loved ones that have passed on, then they could. It's just that easy! Huh, Rick?" "But that just doesn't enter peoples minds. I mean hell, it never would have occurred to me!" I said.

"Anyway guys, my little Charlie's gal later hooked up with this scumbag biker asshole who at first seemed to treat her well enough, even though I thought it was strange that he told little Bunny to not ever call him Dad but to call him Mr. Dick. I mean who does that? How about Richard, that's your name isn't it, asshole? But then the tide turned after a couple of years."

"When my granddaughter, Bunny, turned thirteen this scumbag started showing her a little too much attention, if you know what I mean," Charlie went on to say. "Man, I want him fucking dead!"

"All the while my Charlie and I are, would you call it cursed? I mean having to see all this shit unfold before us and we're helpless to do anything to stop it. So when I set out looking for you, Bob," Charlie said, "I didn't know what to expect, when, or if I ever found you. I only knew I had to do something. I remembered how we looked out for one another and were like brothers back in the jungle, Bob," said Charlie. "Yep, we were like brothers back then," replied Bob. "There's a lot of shit I try to forget about that time in my life but our friendship is not one of them. What can we do to help?" "Hey, Rick, do you have any ideas how we can help old Charlie with his problem?" Bob asked.

"You know guys, I do have an idea swimming around in my head that might just teach this prick a lesson," I told them. "Let me go to my truck to get another cigar and grab another beer from Lenny first. Are you guys ready for another? Just kidding, Bob," I said. "Rick, you're an asshole but I love ya man, go get your freaking cigar," he replied.

When I got back I said, "What I'm thinking is we have to somehow lure "Mr. Dick" up here and get him stinking drunk, and I got an idea on how we can achieve this. Didn't you say he was a biker, Charlie? What kind of motorcycle does he ride?" "Yeah, Rick, he thinks he's in a biker gang and tells people that he is, too, but I know for a fact he's not. And he rides a Harley, that is if you can call that old piece of shit shovelhead he rides a Harley. On a good day it's a rolling junkyard," said Charlie.

"Boys, what we're going to do is send him a letter, telling him somebody put his name in a raffle, for brand new Harley Davidson Road King and he won first prize," I went on to explain. "We'll tell him that to collect on his prize he'll have to show up with three pieces of ID, to this little bar I know of way up country, called Uncle Jesses Cabin." "I know that place," said Bob. "Okay, so then we'll meet up with the second and third place prize winners and from there, after a few drinks, the winners will be taken to a casino in Tahoe to get their prizes and for "Mr. Dick" to get his new scooter."

"My plan is to get him stinking drunk," I continued, "then take him out back and have someone give him the beating of his life. And, if I can get a hold of Danny Spaulding, that used to work for me who's a member, of a real rough California motorcycle club, I think, he would like to talk with that boy." "I think he's going to be in for a real world of hurt. The club Danny Spaulding, rides with does not appreciate anybody impersonating them," I said. "We'll try to set it up in seven to ten days from now. I pray he'll stay away from your granddaughter, Charlie," I said. "Now, go back to your daughter in law's home and keep an eye on him. God bless you my friend."

"Well, Bob, it's been a week since we've seen your buddy. Do you know how we can contact him?" I asked. "Don't you guys have some sort of cosmic hot line or spiritual wave link or something?" "No man, we don't," said Bob, "it's hard enough having to tune out the tortured souls that are all around us let alone try to tune into another displaced soul such as myself, but I'll try. Let me see, oh yeah…Hmmmmm, Ommmmm," Bob chants. "What the hell, Bob. Really?" I asked. "Nah man, I was just yanking your chain, Rick," he says. "He'll be here today; I don't know how I know that, but I do." Sure enough, less than twenty minutes go by and our friend Charlie was standing there next to Bob. "We only have a few hours to spare 'till we're supposed to be at Uncle Jesses Cabin, guys," I said. "We better get this plan in gear."

"Earlier in the day I rented a brand new Cadillac, and a bitchin black tux for the night, so I could pass as the casino limo guy, so I'll go and greet "Mr. Fucking Dick" in the parking lot by his house as planned, and meet you two at Uncle Jesses. Danny Spaulding and a few of his boys will be there waiting. I told Danny there were some picnic tables out back where they could wait and to be sure they parked out of site." "Cool, thanks Rick," said Charlie. "No worries, Charlie, after tonight he'll never hurt Bunny again." "See ya later," I said.

I got to the old strip mall parking lot in south Sacramento where I was to pick up our "Big Contest Winner" at 9:00. As it was just a few blocks from his house I didn't have to wait long; here he comes walking up the street but there's someone with him, ah shit. No, wait a minute, I know who this must be, I thought. As they got closer, without moving his mouth, I heard "Hello, Rick, please don't freak, man. My dad, Charlie Butler, asked me to meet you. I'm little Charlie." Mr. Dick climbed into the backseat as I held the door open for him. I closed the door and made my way around to the drivers side to get in and there was little Charlie standing in front of the car, kind of opaque and fading from view in the headlights. He looked deep into my eyes and just smiled then nodded as if to say thank you, then faded away down the road in the direction he had come.

On the ride up the hill, there wasn't any small talk with that asshole which was a good thing because I didn't have anything to say to this punk, anyway. It was taking everything in me to keep from going over the backseat and beating the shit out of him with the flashlight I had gotten out of the trunk earlier, so the prick could see his way to the door to the Caddy. He just sat back there and drank the free booze and sang along with the radio.

Charlie had told me his favorite type of music was Hank Williams Jr. or any kind of angry white boy rap type shit like that M&M guy, so I had it turned up pretty loud for him from the time he showed his scraggly ass in the parking lot. Damn this guy is ugly!

As I park the car and walk toward the entrance I can see Bob and Charlie standing by the door. "Another drink, Richard?" I asked him. "Sure man, I'll have a double Jack and Coke," he answers. I get him his drink and lead him towards the back door. "Here ya go, pal, lets go out back where we can light up a smoke," I said. Several rounds later he was pretty much toast.

It wasn't long until the "boys" who were sitting on the deck across from us were staring a hole right thru our guest of honor. There were three of them, although I'm pretty sure one would have been enough. As with most wife beaters and child molesters he was just a snake in the grass coward. Danny Spaulding and his boys didn't waste much time before confronting our hero and it wasn't long 'till they started smacking him around just enough until he knew 'who' it was that was doing it. Oh, he knew who it was alright. You could see the fear in this boy's face when he saw the gang's patches on their vests just as clear as you could see his blood, that began to flow from his wounds. All the while Charlie is standing right in front of our boy with a big smile, Bobby standing right by his side, as any good friend would do. Danny tossed me a flashlight and told me to follow him as they picked our guest up off the bench and began walking him into the forest. "Shit, I thought, this is not going to end well." Bob, read my mind and agreed.

We went back about a half mile or so, until the only sounds you could hear were a slight wind and our heavy breathing, plus, the whimpers of our boy Richard. "What are you doing?" I asked. "Shut up, Rick, and just stand over there," Danny told me.

Next thing I knew Richard was stripped of his clothes and tied to a tree, as I watched them take turns smacking him around some more. Then the beating ended and the real torture began as Danny and his boys took turns carving the words, "Child Molester" deep into his chest. Without missing a beat, as if they were a team of short order cooks in a Denny's restaurant, they proceeded to remove the tattoos off of his arms. The big guy they called Tank filleted them off, as clean as a chef in a sushi bar. All the while I stood there frozen and speechless .

"Okay, let's go, we're done here," Danny said. I didn't say a word but just followed them out. I looked back before we got too far away and saw Charlie and Bob standing there looking at that tree. I could swear I saw Richard look Charlie right in the eye and mouth something. I wondered what did he say, could he see Charlie, did he say he was sorry… fuck you, or what?

I followed the trail back to the bar to join Danny and his club brothers and had one last drink for the road. They didn't talk, they just stared at the mirror hanging on the wall behind the bar, and I sure as hell had nothing to say either. After they finished their drinks Danny and his crew, without saying a word, got up and made their way across the road where their bikes were parked. I watched them through the window start them up and leave, I threw down a couple of twenties on the bar and made my way to the door myself.

～

Because Jesse's place is way up country and a little off the grid, as they say, there are no street lights, no sidewalks. Hell, there's two miles of gravel until you get to back to a paved road. I grabbed the keys from my pocket and before I got to the car I felt the overwhelming urge to ask the Lord, to forgive me for my part in this event. I knew in my heart it went too far, but knew there was nothing I could do to stop them once the beating started.

I knelt down at the side of that Cadillac and began to pray as I've never prayed before. As I was asking God to forgive me I looked up and saw Bobby standing there staring at the moon, but he wasn't staring at the moon at all.

～

"Hey, Bob," I said, "I was just asking God"… "Don't say it, Rick," Bob replies, "look there." Standing right in front of the car in the moonlight was what appeared to be an Angel.

The first thing I noticed was an overwhelming burst of warmth that rushed over me, like when you open the oven door to check your dinner and the heat from the oven feels good but makes you immediately back up. In an instant you knew without a doubt this was an agent of the Lord, and he was not happy. This angel, was eight or nine feet tall with, (what I guess was) a wing span of about eight feet wide. It was standing in front of the full moon, and yet, the moon shown through it. The more I looked at it, it seemed to change from something very majestic full of wisdom, to, something very angry, about to teach Bob and I a lesson. I was frightened and spellbound at the same time, as I looked at this vision, I couldn't move. "Is this real, do you see what I see?" I asked Bob.

The angel just looked at us both for what seemed like an hour and slowly shook his head. We both knew, it was not a nod of approval and then as quickly as it appeared it was gone. "Bobby, we should go back and cut him down." "We can't, Rick, he's not there anymore." "What, where did he go and how?" "He, didn't leave on his on, my friend," said Bob, "I saw another visitor before the one, we just witnessed… back at the tree with Charlie."

"Back at the tree while Charlie and I stood there watching Richard die, an angel appeared, only this one was different," Bob explained. "He was just as majestic as the one you and I just witnessed, but this one had a darkness about it. It was clean and beautiful like this one was at first, but then turned scary, dirty, and cold, in fact it was pretty gruesome, ya know?"

"He took Richard first, then he took Charlie. This angel put Charlie under his left wing and Charlie just stayed there, cause he knew running would be a bad idea. Charlie looked up at me and said he was sorry for getting me involved, and then goodbye." "Goodbye Charlie," I told him. "I knew I would never see him again. Richard was placed on his other side, and did not raise his head. Rick, I could see him tremble in fear and cry like a baby. That Vision was also clearly a soldier of the Lord on a mission, but before it left it looked straight in my eyes with such distain, I could no longer look at him, and had to turn away."

"I don't think I'll ever know why it didn't take me, too, Rick, but I gotta tell you my friend…as long as "you" live I hope you never have to see that. Shit, man, I hope I never see that again. I'll never forget that look."

CHAPTER 4.

The Twins

It had been a while since Bob and I had seen each other and my guess is that he needed some time alone, as did I. One thing I know for sure is I'll never step foot in Uncle Jesse's cabin again. Never.

When I was a building contractor all those years life was much simpler. Sure, there was occasional drama with a customer or worker, but for the most part you did your work for the day and then came home to relative peace and quiet. Not so much with my new career as a Private Investigator slash "paranormal problem solver."

Now after I get home from a job either for the state or a private client I can't really talk to Chrystal about my day. This is taking it's toll on me in a totally different way than ever before. I sure as hell can never share any of the adventures Bob and I get into with her, although I'd love to as he was a good friend of hers also. Oh, well, maybe one day I will but until then a cocktail and a good cigar will have to be my leaning post.

As it's now late October, we always take a ride up the coast to the Bodega Bay area which we've been doing for close to 30 years. It's Chrystal's favorite time of year and she just loves this trip. We usually rent a nice home either on the golf course or on the coast and just chill out, eat, and drink for four or five days. I remember years ago we would take a gang of friends with us to play golf at the course right on the coast and do all the other stuff tourists do, but talk about your drama. Shit, there were times when you could just push somebody off a high cliff or at least tell them to pack their bags and get the hell out. So, as of three or four years ago we stopped inviting friends along and just kept it family. Much quieter and safer that way! This year it's just Chrystal, our Saint Bernard Gracie and me.

My lovely wife got a really nice house this year with a great view, she says we've been in this one before, about ten or twelve years ago. After a couple of hours it all came back to me, we stayed there with Bobby and his wife Lorna, you know, the pain in the ass.

∽

So here I am sitting on the deck overlooking the bay with a cocktail in one hand and cigar in the other, just the way I like it. Chrystal's out shopping and I'm about to snuff out my sweet fifty ring Dominican and take a nice nap when I hear, "Hey, Rick, didn't we stay here with you guys a while back?" "You know you did, my friend, that was one of the better trips up here," I said. "Yeah, it was," Bob replied. "The weather was great and we played golf twice that weekend and if I remember right you got what was your longest drive ever." "Man, do I remember that," I said. "I remember, it wasn't my best game but that par four somewhere in the middle of the course, man I really hit the shit outta that ball." "Well, Rick, it was a downhill shot and the ball rolled quite a bit, but you got it almost to the green in that one drive alright." "Hmmm," I said, "it might have rolled a little I guess, huh?"

∽

"What are you doing up here, Bob, and how'd you know we were here?" I asked. "It's late October, Rick, where else would you be? I couldn't forget that. You don't mind if I hang out with you do you?" he asked. "Of course I don't, pal, it's good to see you," I replied. "Tomorrow we'll be taking a ride up the coast hitting a few bars, and antique shops along the way," I said, "you're welcome to join us." "You know I will buddy," said Bob, "but I gotta tell you, Rick, I'm feeling there's a lot of tortured souls here a bouts." "Let's just play it by ear, my friend, and try not to get involved," I replied. "I agree," said Bob.

While making our way, up the Coastal Highway we had to, of course, make all the usual stops like the bakery on the way to the little town of Occidental, and the art studio in the town of Bodega where I sometimes find a gift for my wife. Then there's that funky little bar across the street that has those barbequed oysters. I can see Bobby over there on the bar's front porch. "Whatcha looking at?" Chrystal asked me. "Just looking at the bar wondering if they got those oysters I like so much, Hon?" I said. That and our old friend Bob Moore's spirit hovering from one side of the street to the other, I was thinking.

Out of nowhere and with all the grace of an NFL linebacker Bob gets right in my face and tells me to hurry up and meet him across the street, he's got something he wants to tell me. "Okay," I said, "I'll be right there." "Honey, I'm going over to the bar for a beer." As I started up the old wooden stairs in front of the bar, Bob was at the top of the landing shaking his head from side to side and telling me that this town has a terrible secret.

I made my way inside and ordered a Heineken, with Bob right beside me the whole time explaining how he first heard the screams when we got there but tried to ignore them. There are screams and spirits crying practically everywhere, according to Bob, especially around an old town like this. I remembered Bob had told me shortly after he appeared to me the first time that if a spirit wants you to see them, and at the same time you want to see them, as well, it can be so. The cries and screams he hears are usually because of the sadness people feel when they realize they're in a realm that's neither heaven or hell, but a place where they must relive their past mistakes and really repent and learn from them before they're allowed to go on. But sometimes the screams he hears are because of a terrible tragedy or crime, and that says Bob, will tear your heart out. That type of cry is what he's hearing right now.

Bob, tells me that there were a few local spirits that he overheard on the front porch chewing the fat just as they once did nearly one hundred years ago. I asked him who they were and he explained that they were a couple of local farmers from the valley down the road; the whole area was once occupied by either farmers or fishermen and their families. Unlike today with all the artist types and retired folks moving in. These two old boys had heard the crying and screams, too, and from what I understand, hear it every day. As I nurse my beer I look around and I don't see Bobby at first. Then I looked out the window to see if I could spot him and the two old boys he mentioned. I saw Bobby standing there, but I couldn't see anyone else but Chrystal going into another shop across the way. She saw me and waved, I waved my beer bottle and she smiled.

I ordered another beer, and sat back at the table where Bobby and I were, when he comes back with one of the most interesting, yet sad stories that the farmers had shared with him. Yup, ole' Bobby sure could spin a yarn, as they say, and everyone who knew him knew that if he was a little tight his stories would go on and on with a whole lot of bullshit sprinkled in here and there just for color, or so he thought. "Rick," said Bob, "the old boys out front tell me the cries are coming from a pair of twin boys that lived on a dairy farm just a piece down the road past the first bend, in the year 1910. They lived with their mother and father, the mother's brother, their little sister and a ranch hand. The two boys were born at the same time, which, of course made them twins, but that was as far as it went because one of the boys was what they use to refer to as retarded. Or as one of the old farmers put it, he was a might simple minded."

"Is there anything more, Bob," I asked. "Sure there is, Rick, damn, those two 'ole gents also took me down the road to the Morrison dairy, that was their name, Donnie and Darrell Morrison. And then over to the old town graveyard where I met Mary Beth Sweeney, who knew the family quite well." Bob continued. "Mary Beth, was sweet on Donnie Morrison from the time they were little until the death of the twins (when they were just thirteen years old)." "Wow," I said, "you sure learned a lot in a short amount of time dude." "Remember Rick, different realm, different time frame, yadda, yadda, yadda," Bob replies. "Damn, I'll never get used to that," I reply.

"Well, as Mary Beth tells it she was raised down the road from the Morrison farm and met the twins in the first grade. She went on to say that Donnie was always there for his brother when the other kids would pick on, or make fun of him because he was slow, and different. Donnie taught his brother everything from how to tie his shoes to putting his clothes on and everything in between. There was also their little sister Donna who was five years old back in 1910 when the fire happened. Donnie and Mary Beth had planned to get married one day when they got out of school. The plan was, Donnie was going to work on Mary Beth's fathers fishing boat moored in Bodega Harbor, but both knew that might not ever happen because Donnie had to take care of his brother. But they could dream, and they often did," Bob went on to say.

"Mr. Morrison, along with his brother in law and best friend, Bill, worked that dairy farm from sun up until sun down, like most farmers do. So did

Mrs. Morrison who was only thirty and the perfect farmer's wife. It took her a long time to realize that if it weren't for Donnie, then Darrell would have gone into a state run institution, which weren't very nice back then. The little girl, well you hardly ever noticed her; she was either under the kitchen table, in her room or wandering around the yard. Donna didn't have any friends, just imaginary ones, I guess," Bob said.

"Rick, the tragedy here is that both those boys along with little Donna and their Uncle Bill died when the barn caught fire. The whole town needed to blame someone for the death of those three children so they railroaded the ranch hand, Gus. They never really knew anything about him but like with most small towns, folks gossip. The gossip was Gus came from back east somewhere and rode the rails for years, until the Morrison's took him in. Truth be known, most of the town knew he was innocent but they needed to blame someone, so why not Gus." Bob continued.

"Sure, why not him? God forbid it might have just been an accident with a kerosene lamp. No, he seemed to fit the need, a loner, no family, drinks a bit…perfect fit. So Gus was hanged from a large oak tree in the town square."

"Mary Beth, moved to Santa Rosa to live with her father's sister after grammar school. She grew up, got married, had children and a full, uneventful life right there in Santa Rosa until she died in 1985. She was eighty eight years old. She was buried back here in her family's plot in the Bodega Cemetery. Mary Beth, explained how shortly after the loss of his children and brother in law Mr. Morrison, hanged himself. Mrs. Morrison went insane after her husband's death and was committed and stayed institutionalized until her death in 1988 at one hundred eight years of age. Mother, Father, the three children and Uncle Bill were all laid to rest at Bodega Cemetery. Gus was also buried there, but outside the yard in grave bearing only his first name." Bob told me.

"Rick," said Bob, "It was there in the Cemetery where she was reunited with childhood love, Donnie Morrison. He told her the truth about what happened that day back in 1910. When Mary Beth, was laid to rest there she saw Donnie straight away, on the first day. Although she passed on at eighty eight years of age, to Donnie she still appeared as that lovely thirteen year old girl." "Hey, Bob, here comes my wife so why don't you stop by the house tonight. I think Chrystal's going out for a couple of hours, then you can tell me the rest of the story. I'm very intrigued and have to know what happened," I said. "Sure, Rick, I'll see you later then," Bob replied.

Later that night, my sweetie hooked up with our good friend Cynthia. She's a local, and runs a little art studio in town and we've know her for years. They're going to watch a 'Play' in Santa Rosa, and it's not really my thing. Cynthia, promised to bring her home safely no later than midnight. Yeah, right! Hell, I didn't care how long she stayed out, I trusted my gal. Plus, our friend promised not to drink so she'd be the driver for the night. Bob, showed up as they left and told me there was so much more to the story that he thought it best if I heard it first hand. So off we went to Bodega Cemetery.

On the way there I commented to Bob on how many young hitch hikers there were on the road this late at night and how the moon seem to glow off these kids. Bob told me to look a little closer and see that the glow was from them and not the moon because they were mostly the spirits of hippies from all over America who'd come to California during the 60's and early 70's.

They'd either overdosed on drugs or died in Vietnam or whatever and still dig it here so here they just stay, hitching up and down the coast. "Far out," I said. Bob gave me that look and simply said, "really, dude, far out?"

"Rick," said Bob, "before we get there, I want to fill you in on just who your going to meet tonight and why, you will see them, just as you see me.

First off, you'll meet Mary Beth who's idea it was to set things straight. You'll like her, Rick. Then we'll meet the boys, Donnie and Darrell, who I haven't met yet but Mary Beth's told me all about them, they should be there too." "What about the parents Bob, will they be there? I asked. "I'm not sure Rick, Mary Beth didn't say the would be," replied Bob.

So we pull into the parking lot and make our way to the back corner of the Cemetery, as that's where the really old dated headstones from the 1800's are. We're greeted by the loveliest older lady who instantly reminded me of Aunt Bee from the Andy Griffith Show. "Hellooo, you must be Rick," said this lovely lady with such a glow all around her. "Yes, Ma'am, and you, of course, are Mary Beth," I said. "Let's go over to the bench and sit a spell," said Mary Beth, "I'd like to tell you a story."

As we sit and chat I tell Mary Beth what I already know which is what she shared with Bob earlier that day. "Let me see if I can fill in the holes for you," she says, "do you have any questions Rick?" "Yes, I do," I said, "can you tell me just how the fire started and what exactly happened?"

"Well boys, what I can tell you is what Donnie told me and that is that Darrell was simply playing with matches in the barn and little Donna walked in on him." Bob asked, "what happened then Sweetie?" "Well, boys," said Mary Beth, "as most children would do in that situation, little Donna threatened to tell her daddy which made Darrell very mad. Darrell, picked up the closest thing to him, which was a shovel. He promptly hit his little sister in the head and knocked her out, then to hide the bad thing he had done, Darrell spread cow hay over her, then lit another match." "Oh, my God, no," I said.

"As the fire quickly spread Darrell began to scream hysterically which was heard by Donnie first. Donnie ran in to see Darrell jumping up and down in the middle of the fire with a clear exit to the door, but he was too scared to see it. Donnie told me he yelled and pleaded for Darrell to run to him but he wouldn't. Then Donnie saw why he wouldn't leave, there under smoldering hay lay his little sister Donna, just starting to wake up holding her head and crying. Donnie quickly ran to Donna and snatched her up in his arms, and he also grabbed for his brother's arm to run out of the barn to safety. But it was to late, the exit was now engulfed in flames."

"Uncle Bill, was the next one to hear the screams and was just minutes behind Donnie. He was horrified at what he saw through the barn doors. Bill quickly grabbed a horse blanket and threw it in a water trough, then put it over his shoulders and ran through the flames to save the children. When Bill got inside the ring of fire, Donnie had both Donna and Darrell in his arms, they were on their knees being overcome with smoke. Uncle Bill knew, that all he could do was to hold the children close in his arms, and pray the Lord would not let them suffer. After the fire was put out they found Uncle Bill under all the burnt and charred timbers. The three children, still wrapped tightly in his arms," Mary Beth explained, with a tear in her voice.

"Mr. Morrison, had been in town picking up feed for the cows and heard the fire bells and raced home when he saw the smoke coming from the direction of his farm. When he got to his farm he found his wife passed out laying face down in the mud, not thirty feet from the barn door, her hair and clothing were smoldering from the intense heat. Mr. Morrison sat there in the mud, with his wife in his arms and watched helplessly as the barn burned to the ground."

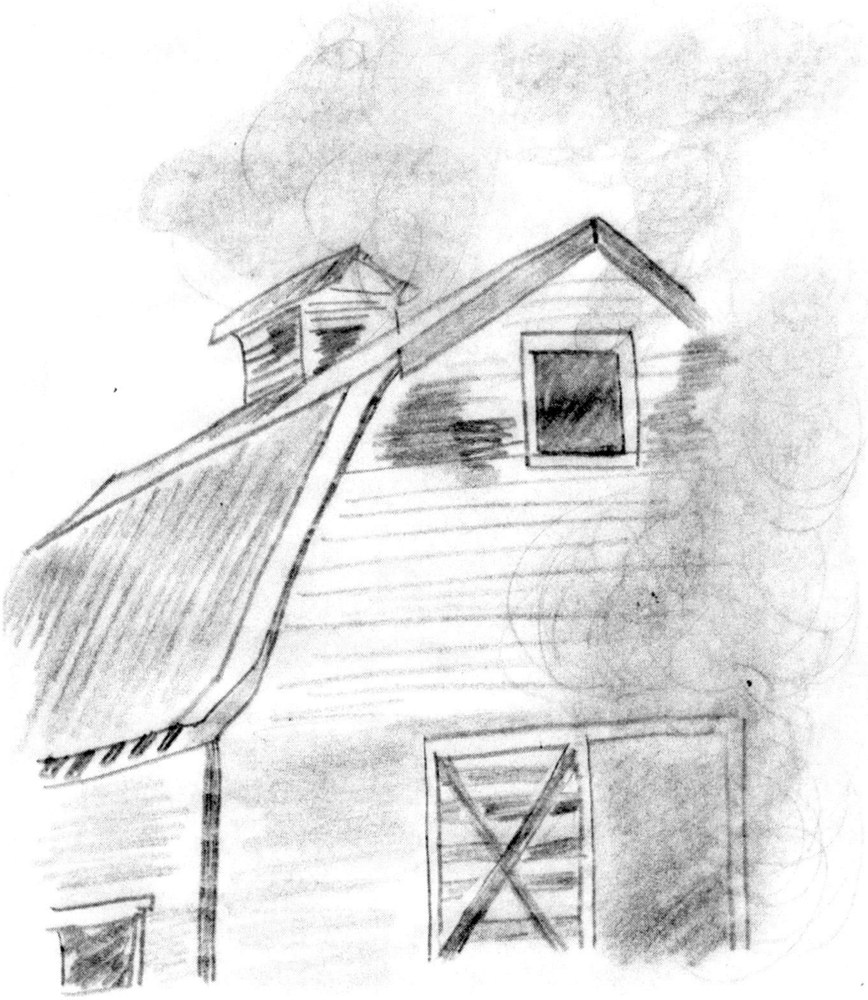

As we sat there on the bench, listening to this horrendous story I could hear someone crying. Bob, and Mary Beth also hear it, and we all turn around to see Mr. and Mrs. Morrison with Uncle Bill standing just a few feet behind us, and over to the left on a hillside outside the Cemetery fence, stands Gus. I was overwhelmed to be a part of this story and started to cry with them, and for them as well. Up until this evening, Mr. and Mrs. Morrison and uncle Bill have been keeping vigilance, at the farm, waiting for the children to appear. These were nice folks, all of them, and I wished that this would have never had happened. I turned to Bobby and smiled with tears rolling down my cheeks and said, "Bob, this is a real gift my friend, thank you." My God, I thought, how can I make this right and let people know the truth?

Just then, the children appeared standing with their Mom and Dad and Uncle Bill. The kids were so happy to be with their family again. Mr. Morrison bent down and picked up little Donna and hugged her ever so tightly. Mary Beth, had walked up the hill and led Gus back down to reunite him with the family. Donnie, and Darrell, both told Gus just how sorry they were, Gus smiled, thanked them and told them, they were forgiven.

I thought to myself, as long as I live our annual trip to Bodega Bay will never be the same. When we got back home and settled in, I sat down at my desk and wrote an anonymous letter to the Sonoma County Gazette. In the letter I told the true story of what had happened that day back in 1910 at the Morrison Dairy farm. My hopes, were that, not only would Bodega history be corrected, but that the grave marked only as "Gus" could be moved inside the Cemetery grounds.

CHAPTER 5.

My Little Fishing Buddy

It's late afternoon, and nice and quiet here on the back deck of the Moonglow Saloon, just the way I like it, although I'm sure Lenny wishes there were a few more thirsty people around. I used to like to come out here to smoke a cigar and watch the occasional horse and rider, or hiker, go by on the trail. Now, I think I enjoy it even more since I've reconnected with my best friend Bob. He may not be here in the flesh but I don't care, he's still the same buddy I once had. Who knows how long this will last so I'm going to appreciate the time we have until that day comes and he's gone again. I feel truly blessed to have my friend back to talk to, I mean how cool is that, to see a dead friend again? It makes me wonder how many other folks there are that talk to their departed friends or family members. You gotta wonder, about all those people walking around with that damn ear piece in "seemingly" talking on the phone, huh? Kinda makes you stop and go hmmmm, doesn't it?

I look over at Bob and he's staring out to the field. "Hey, Bob," I asked, "do you remember when we used to have all those great bands and musicians play here? Those were some great times, eh, buddy?" "Yeah, they were good times alright, some of those bands were fucking great," replied Bob. Just then the juke box starts up, and of course "Reelin in the years" starts to play. "Damn, dude, how do you do that?" I ask Bob, he just shrugs his shoulders and says, "cool huh." "What were we talking about again?" I said, "Oh, yeah."

"Well, it was mostly my wife and the connections she made through the years, but we had a little help from a couple of old friends you might remember," I added. "Do you remember that little Russian guy who used to work for me, Alex Smirnoff, and how good he played the harmonica?" I asked. "Oh man, do I, he could really get down with a mouth harp alright," Bob said. "Well," I replied, "do you also recall that old black guy in the wheelchair that came up with him when we first got the place? called himself, "Cool Poppa" he had a band that played the blues." "Yeah, I do," said Bob. "That's actually when we became friends, I mean, we knew each other and I think I even worked on you wife's car before, but after you guys bought the place is when we really became pals." "Yup, your right," I said.

~

"Man, I'd love to see that little Russian guy again," I said. "You do remember, I told you he drowned in the American River five or six years ago, don't you Bob?" "Yeah, I remember," Bob replies. "I wonder if he's on the same plane as you," I asked. "Do you think maybe you could get the word out like you did before on that "spiritual grape vine" you folks use, and find him for me?"

"God forbid, he's burning in hell somewhere. He had his faults but he had a really big heart and was a pretty good guy. Can you help me find him Bob?" "Sure, Rick, I'll see what I can do," said Bob. "Did I ever tell you what a good fisherman he was, Bob?" "Little guy liked to fish, did he?" said Bob. "Yeah man, every chance he got. Hell, I never really saw the attraction of it until I met him and he took me salmon fishing."

"He helped me land a thirty eight pounder; damn thing took forty five minutes to bring in. Man, I gotta tell ya, it sure was fun." "Wow, that was a big fish," says Bob.

The next day while driving up to Placerville to talk to a client good 'ole Bob appears in the passenger seat. "Morning Rick." "Morning Bob." "Hey Rick, guess who I ran into last night at the monthly "Spirits" meeting?" said Bob. "What, monthly what? Are you kidding me?" I replied. "Sure, of course you wouldn't know about it, I mean how could you? You'll first, have to be, you know…dead. Then, of course, there's the clubhouse where we meet and greet each other with the secret hand shake, and you damn sure better not forget your 'Old Ghosts Rule' hat, and tee shirt," Bob goes on to say. "Alright asshole, you had me going there for a while until you got to the secret hand shake. So, who'd you hook up with?" I asked. "Well, just look in your rear view mirror and see for yourself." "Holy shit, is that you Alex?" I asked. "Hi, Rick. Man this is weird, I didn't know this was possible 'till your friend Bob found me and explained," said Alex. "Yeah, I found him wandering up and down the banks of the river watching the fish, and trying to get into all the fishermen's coolers every time he saw a cold beer come outta one," said Bob.

"I've already filled him in on all the reasons why he's here in this place and gave him the quickie course on what, and how to do shit here, because there's no one to help you figure it out, but yourself." "Damn, I wish there would have been someone to show me the ropes," said Bob. "Thanks, Bob," I replied. "It was pretty cool of you to hunt him down for me. Maybe now he'll stop wandering around old fishing spots and move on." "Alex," I said, "your wife called us after they found your body down river. Buddy, can you tell me what the hell happened to you? That was your favorite spot, and you were a first class angler and swimmer, what the hell happened?"

"Well, Rick, remember that guy I went to work for after you moved up to the foothills?" asked Alex. "You mean that asshole with the temper you called and told me about," I said. "Yeah him," replied Al. "Well, he was always bragging to me about how great of an angler he was so I thought I'd take him down to that spot below the Hatchery. Salmon season had just started and I was aching to go myself," said Al." "Yeah, that's where you and I always went," I replied.

"Well, Rick, every local angler knows that if you can't catch a fish there then you just can't catch a fish. You, of course didn't need luck, or skill there, you had me. I mean, when the season first opens the river is so full of fish you can almost walk to the other side on their backs." "So what happened, man," I asked. "This guy just couldn't catch a fish huh?" "No, man, I never seen anything like it, he really sucked at fishing. Shit, he wasn't much of a builder, either, unlike you Rick. The only thing he was good at was bullshitting people. He would get these jobs and expect his crew to lay it out and build it, lazy bum hardly ever put his tool belt on. You could always find him at the nearest bar around noon. I mean, he expected his crew to do everything, and to make him look good. Always promising bonuses too, but he never gave out a fucking dime. What a jerk," Alex explained. "So again, I'm asking, WHAT THE HELL HAPPENED?" I asked, rather loudly.

"Well, you know me, Rick," said Alex. "I caught my limit within the first half hour and then tried to help him but he didn't want any help. I mean, he had all the right gear; top of the line rod and reel, a hundred dollar fishing vest, and that stupid KC Royals baseball cap he always wore because, he had the same initials. What a bozo. Anyway, I just kept catching and releasing and drinking beer, then out of left field he picks a fight with me about nothing." "Excuse me for a minute, Alex," I said. "Hey, Bob, you know me from the bar days and know when somebody was being picked on, or in trouble, I most always step in. Well, in all the years Alex and I ran together I would sometimes have to step in and help him out," I said. "I mean forgive me Alex, but "dude," you always drank to much and quite often had a big mouth buddy." "Yeah, I know, but that's not what happened this time, Rick, I swear, I didn't say a word to start shit, all I did was try to help him catch a damn fish, really!" said Alex.

"Anyway, he was in my face and it was getting dark and cold. I was getting a little drunk, and he just kept getting in my face. I finally couldn't take it anymore and pushed him away, and told him to back off. Then, like a mad man he grabbed me by my beard, so I grabbed at him, too. Only I grabbed his stupid hat off. Then outta nowhere he smacked me in the head with a full bottle of Miller Lite; he had in his vest." "Whoa, what happened next?" I asked. "Well, it knocked me right off my feet and into the water and my waist high waders filled with water so fast it pulled me down."

"That must have been really scary, Al," I said. "Ah, man, I remember fighting and struggling to get to the bank but it was just so hard, and I was getting tired. Those waders with all that water in 'em, it was just too hard. I remember my last thought was to stop struggling because I finally realized I couldn't win, so just let the current take me and maybe I would get lucky and catch a log or somebody would see me and help. At one point, before I got to far away I was able to get my head outta the water, and look right at him," said Alex. "Oh, and did he look back at you?" I asked. "You know guys, he looked right at me and just opened another beer," replied Alex. "That low life, heartless, mother fucker," I replied.

"Wow, what happened then Alex?" Bob asked. "All the while I was tumbling, and gasping for a breath, but all I was getting was more water in my mouth. I kept going under and hitting my head on every fucking rock in the river until, the water got real calm, and it was over." "Damn, buddy," I said.

"Next thing I knew, I was standing on the bank of the river under the Watt Avenue bridge. I stared at myself floating in the water, face up still holding on to that stupid fucking hat."

"I guess, it was a couple of miles down river from where we were fishing. The next day, a homeless guy who was living under the bridge found me and pulled me up onto the bank, I went with him when he called 911 from a pay phone, that was nice."

"It was funny, at first he climbed up the hill to the roadway and tried to flag down a car but of course no one would stop for this poor dirty homeless guy, so that's when he went to the pay phone at the 7/11 store. It was about a mile away. He's a real nice guy, too, you'd like him, Rick," said Alex.

"I followed him around for I think a couple of days and watched him look for work, and gather cans and bottles along the roadway. I even scared a couple of fish his way, too, at least I'd like to think I did. But then I thought about where I died and if anybody picked up my cooler and jacket and stuff, as quick as I thought of it, I was there. Weird, huh," said Alex. "Not weird at all," replied Bob. "What else strikes you as weird?" "Well, I was at the river where you found me, and one day, it must have been about noon. I remember, this nice family was getting ready to eat their lunch at the picnic table by the parking lot, and I was thinking about my brother and sisters and "poof" I was there at my sister's house. Kind of cool, huh guys," said Alex. "Yeah, it must be," I said. "But then I came back to my spot on the river after what I thought was just a few minutes at my sister Nina's house, and that same family was packing up their car in the parking lot. The sun had gone done and it was getting dark. It seemed like only a few minutes went by for me, now that is weird, huh, guys?"

"So, Alex," I said, "you showed up at your own wake, at your sister Nina's house. How did it feel to be in the same room with your family as a spirit?" I asked. "It was a sad day alright, my mother and father just sat there holding pictures of me, sobbing and holding each other. My brother, and his girlfriend and my sisters were eating and drinking and sharing stories about me. Man, there was a lot of food, Russian food. Remember, Rick, those blitzes my mother used to make?" "Yeah man, they were great," I said. "And it was really strange to see those three old ladies I'd never seen before screaming and crying in the hallway, until I remembered that was tradition. My parents, must have gotten them to come up from the Russian Church. I'll bet the neighbors were glad when that party ended."

⁓

"So, dude, what do you do with yourself now? Do you understand why you're stuck here, or there, where you are?" I asked. "Not really, and I don't know if I even care, Rick. I mean, my life was really shit anyway. All I did for years was basically just work and get high, work and get high, and of course, go fishing," said Alex. "Now I spend most of the day watching people fishing. Sometimes I hang out with my new buddy, Roger." "Who's that?" I asked. "You know, the guy that pulled me out of the river," he says. "Why?" I asked. "I don't know," replies Al, "he's a really nice guy, he's just down on his luck. Man, he sure could use a break, but nobody wants to talk to him or even be around him let alone hire this smelly, unkempt, homeless guy."

"I mean shit, he used to have a good job, a wife and a kid, and a nice home. Then he got laid off and one day, his wife took the family SUV out with their little boy and never came back. Fucking bitch, huh guys?" "So, you like this guy Roger, eh buddy?" I asked. "I do," he said. "I think I'll hang out with him for a while." "He's a pretty good angler and fun to watch, too." "What about this guy you used to work for that hit you in the head with a beer bottle?" asked Bob.

⁓

"Yeah, what about him?" I asked. "And who the hell is this guy?" "His name is Kenny Collins, KC Construction," said Alex, "he lives in Rancho Cordova but hangs out at the San Juan Club in our old neighborhood, Rick." "You know, Alex," I said, "I don't build anymore. I studied and got a license to be a private investigator a couple of years ago. If you don't mind, what the hell am I saying, even if you DO mind I'm going to find this guy and make him pay for what he did." "Okay, Rick, I don't mind. Why would I mind? I've always trusted you man, we were like brothers, weren't we," says Al. "We were pals, yes, and still are, and if I have to beat the shit out of this guy myself he's going to pay for what he did to you." "Hey, Bob, can you save me some time and find this piece of trash for me?" I ask. "I can do that," says Bob. "Let's get on over to the Moonglow and have a beer. Oh, that's right you guys can't. Well, I'll have an extra one, and tell you how good it was." I said. "Hey, Alex," says Bob, "was he always a horse's ass like this?"

As we sit on the back deck of the bar I notice that Alex looks a little nervous and can't keep still. "What's the matter, buddy?" I ask. "Man, since Bob gave me more insight on things I want to go back home and visit my family again," Alex replies. "It's not that easy, Alex," says Bob, "I want you to really listen to me because I think you got the wrong idea, dude. What I said was that the person you want to see, has to REALLY be thinking of you with all their heart, and the timing has to be just right for you to be able to appear to them. It does not always happen, hell, if it did there'd be a party going on in the spirit world all the time, instead of the grief and sorrow that really exist here." Bob goes on to say, "you're HERE in this place to learn from your mistakes, man, please for your own good, don't ever forget that." "I won't, Bob, and thanks," says Alex, "but I'll never know unless I try. I'll remember the stuff you taught me, and I'll see you guys later. Oh, and Rick, it's good to see you man." "You too pal, now that you know where I am, don't be a stranger and come back and visit soon."

As the day wears on I start to get really tired and a little head achy. "What's wrong, my friend?" asks Bob, "You don't look so good." "Hell, I don't know Bob, probably just a little too much stress. I mean it's hard enough solving your own troubles let alone the troubles of dead folks," I said. "Nobody asked you to get involved, Rick, you took that on yourself." "I know man, but what the hell was I supposed to do after hearing that story? I tell ya man, I loved that little guy," I said. "Then do what you gotta do, Rick," replies Bob.

A serious look crosses Bobs face and he starts to tell me. "Rick, there is something I've been wanting to tell you, pal. I just recently noticed, what is happening to you. Something is wrong with you, I'm not sure what it is but I Know it's not good." "What do you mean?" I replied. "You seem to have what looks like a dark growth on the back of your head, I think you better get it looked at real soon," says Bob. "I can't feel anything," I said. "It's at the base of your brain, Rick, and it's nothing to fuck around with, I'm sure of that," Bob says. "How long have you had this ability to see sickness in somebody Bob?" "Just a couple of days now, weird huh?" "You think?" I said. "Well shit, I have to find this guy Kenny first and set him straight, then I'll go to the doctor and have it looked at." "You better," says Bob, "or I'll haunt you the rest of your life. If you don't get it taken care of and this thing kills you, which it will, you'll be here with me and I'll make your existence here a living HELL. You got that, dude?" "Got it, Bob, just as soon as we take care of this piece of shit, Kenny what's his name. And Thanks man, I love you too."

Bob, finds our boy without any problem and we both head on down to the San Juan Club in Sacramento, his favorite hang out. As I step inside the place I notice it's still the same dump it was all those years ago, when I lived in the area. It still smells like a dirty ashtray too. Bob, is right in front of me and points the dude out, he kinda looks familiar but I can't place him just yet. I'm thinking to myself, I'm going to sit right next to him.

"No don't, sit at the end of the bar and be more subtle," says Bob. "WTH, you can talk to me telepathically now? When did this happen and is there anything else you want to share?" I thought. "Cool huh, Rick, now you don't have worry about looking like a fool talking to yourself," replies Bob.

After some small talk with the old barmaid about me having lived in the area before, and of course, whether or not I was married, I made my way over to the pool table. "Try not to make eye contact with her," says Bob "and maybe she'll hit on somebody else." "Good advise, I'll look at the floor when ordering next time," I replied.

"Anybody want to play a game?" I said loud enough for everybody to hear. To my good fortune our boy struts over and says to me, "sure, I'll play. I'm Kenny," he said. "Yeah, I know who you are, Kenny Collins right?" I said. "Real subtle Rick," says Bob. "Do I know you?" he ask me. "I don't think so pal, but I know you," I replied. "And how's that?" he asked. "Well, a good friend of mine used to work for you, his name was Alex, Alex Smirnoff, you remember him, don't you pal? He's dead now, but you know that too, right?" "Yeah, I knew him, he worked for me on a couple of jobs," he says. As I rack the balls I looked him right in the eye and said, "I know, he told me. He also told me you guys went fishing together." About this time Bob is staring a hole straight through our boy as he pauses and says, "no, I never went fishing with him." "My game, my break," I said. As I smack the balls and they spread over the table he looks over the spread and I say, "yes you did, pal. On opening day of salmon season back in '04 when he went missing." "What are you taking about?" he replies. I put my hand on his cue stick with grip that a pro hockey player would be proud of and reply, "look, asshole, we can play this game all fucking day, until I'll eventually have to kick the living shit out of you. So let's stop all the bullshit, and I'll tell you that I know, what you did. Oh, hey, I see you still enjoy the same beer as the one you smacked poor Alex in the head with."

Our boy, about chokes on the last swallow of his Miller Lite as he sits the bottle on the edge of the pool table and simply says, "I'm outta here man, thanks for the game." Bob tells me that he's been to Kenny's truck and warns me about the nine millimeter pistol under the seat. "Look jackass, before you run off and hide," I said, "let me tell you what's going to happen. First of all, you probably don't know Alex's older brother, Nikko, do you? Well, I do and I know he happens to be a soldier in the Russian Mafia, and I also know for a fact that he misses his little brother quite a bit. I wonder what he would do if he all of a sudden he came into possession of your old KC Royals ball cap?" Kenny squints a bit and looks down at the floor. "That's right, Kenny, I got your ball cap. Do you catch my drift pal?" I said. "So, I'm giving you ONLY one choice to make here if you want to live, and that is to do the right thing and turn yourself in, and I mean right fucking now, today. You have one hour."

"How the fuck do you know any of this anyway?" Kenny ask me. "Never mind how I know asshole, just know that I do," I said. "Oh, and make sure you tell the sheriff about the nine millimeter under your seat too." It was the dear in the headlights stare coming my way, from our boy for at least a very uncomfortable three minutes, until I had to finally add." "Kenny," like I said, "you got one hour to get your good for nothing happy ass to the Sherriff's department, so you better get moving. I got Nikko on speed dial," as I show him my phone with Nikko S. on the screen. "I'm debating, whether to just call him anyway."

~

As he makes his way out to his truck I was wishing that Bob could have removed that gun, but we all know that a spirit can't pick up a solid object. Hell, if so Bob would probably be sipping on a vodka cranberry right about now. But our boy just gets in his rig, takes one last look at me in the doorway and drives off up San Juan Avenue in the direction of the Sherriff's office.

Bob tells me to finish my beer and have another if I want to, he'll follow Kenny for a bit and then come back. Bob came back about twenty minutes later and informed me "all's well that end's well." "What's that, a saying from an old movie?" I ask. Bob, smiles, and tells me that Kenny sat in his truck in the parking lot for awhile until a couple of officers came out and asked him what his business was. "So, he's in jail?" I asked. "Yeah man, he told them the whole story and he's now a resident of the state of California. "Lets get the hell out of 'crazy town' and get back home, Rick." "You know it, brother, I hate it down here, lets go," I said. "So what's the brother, Nikko, really do?" Bob asked. "I think he sells water purifying kits somewhere in the bay area," I replied. "And the phone number in your directory?" "Well, I had to have a number with a bay area prefix, so this one, I believe, is a Russian Tea House somewhere in San Mateo." "Good thinking, dude, just in case he called your bluff, huh?" asked Bob.

"Hey, man, before we head back up the hill, I want to stop by the Watt avenue bridge. I want to see if Alex's new friend (Roger) is still there, and if he is, I'm going to make a few calls to try and help him out." "You're a good man, Charlie Brown," said Bob.

On the way back up the road to the foothills where it's a whole lot quieter Bob says, "my gut feeling, Rick, is that your little fishing buddy never gave a shit, whether Kenny ever saw justice for what he did or not." "Yeah, I get that too," I replied. "Hey Bob, I'm not trying to undo all the wrong I see, I just want to make things right when I can." "The man upstairs knows that Rick, he knows," Bobby said.

Back at the Moomglow it seems there's a little problem. Lenny, the owner, comes over to me just as soon as I step through the door and tells me that the band he hired to play refuses to take the stage. It seems that their little chick singer who claims to be part "Gypsy" says there's no room on the stage because it's crowded with spirits!" "Come on, really?" I said to Lenny.

I look over at the stage to see Bobby on the dance floor dancing like he used to with an imaginary cocktail in one hand trying not to spill it, and pretending to have a cigarette in the other. Man, this is some funny shit. Then I look up, and all at once they appear to me, there's Cool Poppa sitting in a chair playing guitar, Alex blowing on a mouth harp, and a half dozen other musicians on drums, sax, horn, and a couple more on guitars, jamming away to a real bluesy version of, Steely Dan's "Reelin in the Years." Man, this is cool I think to myself, as I wave to Poppa, Alex and the boys. I look at Bob, dancing his heart out and ask, "you requested this song didn't you?" Bob just nods his head up and down, smiles and keeps dancing.

"Why are you swaying back and forth Rick?" asked Lenny, "The juke box has been broken all week." "Oh, just a tune in my head, brother. Hey send the Gypsy over to me, will ya," I replied. I stepped out to the back deck and was followed by this cute little olive skinned gal with what has to be premature long gray hair 'cause she looks to be only thirty. "Hi, are you Rick?" she asked, "I'm Sabrina."

⸻

Of course you are, I was thinking to myself. "Hi, yeah, I'm Rick," I say. "Hey listen, Lenny told me of your concerns and I can fully understand but." "You can see them, can't you?" she asked me. After a couple of very uncomfortable and awkward moments, it kinda felt like getting caught by a highway patrolman with your pants down taken a piss along the side of the road. "Don't deny it," she said, "I can see it in your eyes. And you see that little fat guy with the baseball cap turned backwards dancing in front of the stage, too, don't you?" As I was about to spill the beans and share my new gift with her, Bobby tells me the boys are just about to wrap it up so tell her there's nothing to worry about. "Okay I will," I replied, "kicking up your heels a bit in there, were you, buddy?" "Yeah, man, you know I used to love to dance, I guess I still do." I tell her to take another look at the stage, which is now empty. Sabrina smiles and shakes her finger at me and says, "oh, you're, the sly one."

Alex, Poppa and his boys have made their way to the front of the building. Alex is pushing Poppa's wheelchair with a brand new step now that he has his friends to keep him company. It's good to see him happy, even if he is a spirit. So off they go, arm in arm like Dorothy and her gang of misfits from OZ, the merry "Spirit Blues Band," marching down the road. Or should I say gliding two feet above the road, turning only once to wave goodbye. Bob and I wave back. Safe journeys, little buddy…

CHAPTER 6.

The Orange Man

I still sometimes find myself wondering whether I'm living in a dream or not. I mean, can this really be for real? Are there others out there that have had a similar encounter, and if so, where the hell are they? Man, it's just downright exhausting at times. Not the being able see and communicating with my departed friend, no, I really love that. It's never knowing what the next dilemma might be and always being put in the position to be some poor souls last resort to redemption. Not that I'm complaining, mind you, I'd like to think I'm not made that way although we all complain a little. No, it's just the stress of wanting to help those that really deserve it and making the bad guys pay for what they did is, as I said, exhausting at times. Makes you wonder how a judge can sit on the bench for years, and have to deal with all the shit that comes across his desk don't it?

It shouldn't be hard to float my workload over to the next guy on the list of state approved private investigators. Putting all the states politics that I'm not to fond of aside, there's one thing I gotta say for them, they do pay on time and they seem to understand the need for an occasional holiday in this line of work. So, every now and then, I just have to have a little "me" time and get away for a bit. A trip back to the east coast to show my granddaughter Washington, DC, might be nice and who knows, maybe see a few old friends, while we're there.

As I stop by the Moonglow to let Lenny know I'll be out of town for a while I see Bobby standing at the back window staring out across the field out back.

"Hey, Bob, whatcha doing, pal?" "Oh, hi Rick," he replies, "I'm just trying to figure it all out, man." "What's that, Bob?" I ask. "Well," he says, "I've been dead according to you for almost five years now, and I just don't know what to think, Rick. I made some mistakes sure, who didn't, so why am I still here? What am I suppose to learn from this? I mean shit man, we've helped others move on, when's it going to be my turn?" "I don't know, my friend." I said, "but if it's any comfort to you, I sure dig having you around again. I really missed you, Bob, and when you appeared to me a several months ago I felt like a little kid having the best day ever, with his best pal. So, I hope you're not leaving anytime soon." "I think I'm here for a while yet, Rick," said Bob. "What's up?"

"I got to get away, Bob," I said. "I'm thinking of taking the wife and the little one back east, and maybe go to D.C. and visit a few sites around Baltimore. I wanted to know if you'll join me, could be interesting. What do you think?" "Yeah, why not," Bob replies, "are you going to visit your sister again?" "Sure I will, be kinda hard to be in Baltimore without stopping by for a visit. I think I'll give her a call this time to let her know we're coming."

Lenny, comes down to the end of the bar where Bob and I were chatting and asked if I'd like to get in a quick golf game at the little nine hole course across the street. "Sure," I say, "I have my clubs in the truck." Bobby comes along, because there's nothing he likes better than golf. Boy, I think to myself, I really miss playing golf with Bob. Well, he may be gone but at least I'll have the advantage of his expertise, ha, if only Lenny knew I got a ringer in my pocket.

On the third hole, I was about to tee off when I heard that distinctive crack of a club making contact with a ball, and it was coming from right behind us. Just as I turned to see where that ball was, I saw it heading straight for Lenny's head. The next thing that happened still blows my mind. It happened so quick, but seemed to happen one frame at a time, in slow motion. I guess you could say that time stood still for a moment.

Bobby, moved straight through Lenny like he was made of smoke. He reached up and grabbed that ball an instant before it hit Lenny, stopping it dead in it's path. The ball now in Bob's hand seem to be suspended for a moment, then it simply dropped to the ground. Sparring Lenny one hell of a headache or worst. "Damn, Bob, that was fantastic," I said. Ah shit, did I just say that out loud, I thought. "yeah you did," replied Bob. "What, where, Bob?" Lenny said. "Didn't you see that?" I asked Lenny. "No," Lenny replied, "see what?" Bobby looks at me, shakes his head and says, "No, Rick, now's not the time." After I tell Lenny about the ball that almost hit him, we both decided it must have been just an optical illusion. Now our attention turns to tee box number two, and we see four young, cocky guys standing there. Oh man, I think to myself, Lenny looks pissed.

"Lenny," I said, "I think I need a drink right about now, how about you?" "Yup, that's a good idea Rick, lets go." We grab our bags and walk straight up the middle of the fairway never taking our eyes off the four assholes standing on the tee box. As we arrive at their tee box those four golfers went silent. And just like little kids who've been busted for screwing something up or breaking something, just stared towards the ground. They were maybe mid to late twenties, and not feeling so tough now that Lenny and I were standing right in front of them. "Who hit that ball?" I ask, as both Lenny and I drop our bags to the ground. They're now looking up at these two big mean looking, angry, old guys. You can smell the fear in the air, or was that the overflowing garbage can behind them, in any case they looked worried.

Bobby's, standing right in front of this one guy and poking him in his chest saying, "this is the jerk right here, Rick." The guy with tattoos on his neck man's up and says, he's sorry, he didn't think it would go that far. Lenny, and I look at each other, and give them 'the stare,' (you know, like the way you look at a guy who don't move, when the traffic light turns green) for a few moments. This made it even harder for them to make eye contact so, I thought I'll end this bullshit, and said to Lenny, "lets go have that drink." Lenny, tells them to be more careful, and they all say they're sorry once again. At the bar Lenny asked me, why I yelled out to Bobby? I explained, that I was just thinking about him, and that was all. I asked Lenny, "how was it that you were able to stay so calm today with those morons?" Lenny replies, "you know, Rick, in my parents house where I grew up there was a portrait of Jesus in the hall right next to a picture of John Wayne. My dad had this thing he would do whenever a problem arose." "Yeah, what was that Len?" I asked. "He would always say, what would Jesus and John Wayne do? and nine times out of ten, that would calm him down."

"And the one time in ten?" I replied. "Not much to say to that, buddy, dad always did the right thing," Lenny answered. "Way cool my friend, way cool," I said.

I have another drink then head home to get ready for the trip in the morning.

∽

After we relax at the hotel for a bit and freshen up we make it over to my sister's house. I'm pleasantly surprised to find her standing on the front porch looking better than I've seen her in a long time. Bobby, tells me my Mother is standing right behind her, looking as lovely as always. "What are you smiling about honey?" Chrystal ask me. "Just happy to be here, hon, and don't Linda look good?" As Chrystal makes her way up the walk, Peanut runs ahead to hug her Aunt Linda. As I open the trunk to get our gift we brought along, I hear Bobby, and his voice is trembling.

Even with our new telepathic ability I can hear the change in his voice. "What's the matter, my friend?" I ask. "It's your Mother, Rick," he replies. "When your granddaughter passed by your mom, your mom reached out for her. Rick, you could feel the love coming from your mom like a warm summer afternoon. I wonder if the little one felt anything? And Rick, there was a glow all around her like I've never seen, we're her eyes, blue?" "No, they weren't," I said. "God, I wish I could see her." "She's smiling at you now, Rick," Bob shared, as I walk up the stairs. Which makes me tear up, even now. "Oh honey, you're my big emotional man, aren't you?" says Chrystal. "Yeah, I guess." Hi Mom, I love you," I whispered, as we walked through the door.

As we sat and had a nice visit and ate some killer crab cakes with a few frosty adult beverages, I couldn't help but catch a story on the local news about an old unsolved case, that they air around every Halloween. It was about some crazy dude that terrorized this section of town called Claremont back in the 50's and 60's. His name was Frank Kirby and he was a resident of Claremont, they called him the "Orange Man." Fact was, according to local history there was a short time in the early 50's when the Orange Man first started terrorizing kids, on Halloween night.

I read that the attacks had stopped, so for a while, it gave little kids and their parents a false sense of security, on Halloween (that didn't last long). After three or four years that crazy bastard, seemed to come out of retirement and start up right where he left off.

It couldn't be the same guy, I said to myself, they found him dead. "Linda do you remember the story of the Orange Man from the time we lived in the Projects?" I asked.

"Not really, Rick, but I've heard about it," she says. "I remember," Gus said. "I always thought it was one of those urban legends, you know, like the Boogie Man or that Pumpkin Head guy down south or something. That's also, about the time when that little girl went missing," adds Gus. "Did they ever find her," I asked. "No, I don't think they ever did," said Gus. "Anyway, they found this guy in Claremont only after the neighbors called the police because no one had seen him for days. I guess the mail, was pouring out of his mailbox and the smell coming out of his apartment was pretty bad." "I guess that could only be one thing, huh? So what did they say on the news about the old guy?" I asked.

"Well," said Gus, "I guess they found dozens of old shopping bags with Halloween pictures colored on them with crayon like we used to do, remember Rick?" "I sure do," I said. "We didn't go to the store and buy a plastic pumpkin for trick or treating. Back then we always took a brown paper grocery bag and decorated it. I remember, some of the real greedy kids would use a pillow case." "Man, remember how big the candy bars were back then?" said Gus. "Well anyway, the Baltimore Sun paper article said that there was crayon colored pictures and old dried blood on practically all of those bags. There was also a few Halloween masks, and a closet full of old candy wrappers plus the orange outfit he used. It was folded up nice and neat and stored in a wooden case under his bed, along with a few snapshots of the same little boy in Halloween costumes, at what looked like a farm somewhere," Gus explained.

"He'd been dead for some time according to the newspaper," Gus said, "and I guess they don't really know anything about the old boy either. You know, where he came from or if that's him in the snapshots, is there any family, where is that farm, something, anything… The Sun paper said the police are really stumped," adds Gus.

"What do you mean? He was a loner, a hermit type of character who never bothered anybody, just paid his rent on time and wanted to be left alone. Shit, nowadays that describes a lot of people. But back then that would be the first guy in the neighborhood they should have looked at," I said. "I guess the neighbors said he never came out of his house, after his father died. He put all his bills in the mailbox outside his door and had everything delivered. You could do that back then, everything from milk, food, liquor, cigarettes, laundry, hell anything," said Gus.

"Yeah, all I know is he was for real alright, because I saw him one time as he ran into the woods. Man, that really scared the piss out of me, I haven't thought about that in almost fifty years. Wow, that sure feels strange to say that," I explain.

"I'm pretty sure I've heard the story about the little girl Rick, but can you tell it to me again?" asked Linda. "Sure, no problem hon, you were to little to go trick or treating at night so maybe that's why you don't remember. He only came out on Halloween night and by then Mom, Tony or Paul were usually home to watch you so Jon and I could go out. Anyway, here goes."

"After our father, 'that prick,' left us back in 1957 or '58, I think, yeah '58, Mom had to move us to a place she could afford. You know, the poor part of town they called the projects? Hell, I thought it was nice, but what did I know, I was just six or seven years old. Anyway, the place was called Claremont. Hey, Gus, is that place still there?" I asked. "Yeah, it's still there Rick, only it went through a major renovation in the early 2000's Gus explained. It's a lot nicer now, shit, you couldn't walk through there in the daytime let alone at night. You'd be taking your life in your hands." "Well, it was sort of old when we lived there but a decent enough place," I said. As we were there visiting I looked around for Bobby and he was nowhere in sight. Hmm, I thought, he must be checking out the night life in the city of Baltimore. "So anyway, like I was saying about Claremont…"

"It was a big place, maybe 300 to 400 apartments and townhouses with one main road that went right down the middle of it, with little courtyards and a couple of side streets. There was a community center and a baseball field, plus a wooded area where we use to play army and climb trees and build forts and things like that," I said. "Hey, Rick, tell us about the Orange Man already, jeez," says Linda.

"Alright, don't get your panties in a bunch," I said, "so every Halloween just as soon as it got dark, and man, when you're a little kid it got dark and scary real quick. Anyway, the best way to get from one group of houses to another was on this sidewalk that bordered the wooded area. That area went down to the ball field. As it got darker kids would start to hug the side of the walkway close to the houses, kind of like when you have to go down in the basement to turn out a light, and you run back up the stairs hugging the wall just in case there's a monster under the stairs."

"Man, when I think back it must have been a funny site, all those screaming kids running up and down the sidewalk. When it got dark there was only a single file line to one side and everybody fighting to keep their place, because you dare not walk on the side close to the woods 'cause that's where the Orange Man was, in the woods."

"He was a big guy too, as I remember, well over six feet tall and maybe two hundred pounds. He would jump out of his hiding spot and grab at your bag of candy. Only he wouldn't just grab, he had a straight razor he would slash out with wildly, while trying to get that bag of candy. We always thought he was trying to cut the handles off your bag. But he always cut some poor kids hand or arm instead, he even cut a kid's face one year. They called him the Orange Man because he wore an orange ski mask, orange sweats, orange gloves and sneakers. Man, you had to be pretty brave to walk that path Halloween night."

"I remember, some older guys one year thought they would try to catch him. A group of maybe, six or seven teenagers and dads patrolled up and down the sidewalks with baseball bats and lead pipes, but they never got a glimpse of him. We lived their from 1958 until '61 and I would never have even thought of walking that pathway by myself, even after Halloween was over. I'd only do it now in daylight, and with a gun in my pocket," I said.

"So Gus, as I remember it the Orange Man's reign of terror stopped back in the early 60's didn't it?" I asked. "Yeah, it all ended in the early to mid 60's, Rick," replied Gus. "Hmmm, I'm thinking Bobby and I should look into this." "I'm, one step ahead of you, Rick," says Bob, who's now standing right beside me. "Dude, you gotta give me a little heads up before you do that," I thought.

"Do what, just appear to you?" says Bob. "There ain't nothing I can do about that Rick, when I think it, it just happens, so get over it already," Bob says. "Oh yeah, and before I went out sightseeing around this very interesting city of yours, I was right beside you and saw that story on T.V., and I felt an overwhelming need to find the place they call Claremont." As I think to myself, I wonder what happened to that little girl back in '61? Bobby's right there in my thoughts and tells me that he's found someone who knows. "Let's get together in the morning and I'll share what I know with you," says Bobby. "Cool, I'll see you in the morning then, good night, Bob."

I get up early and go down to the hotel restaurant for coffee and step outside for my morning cigar and Bobby appears to me. "Rick," he says, I found the Projects you use to live at and came upon a few spirits in the area that would talk with me." "Oh," I said, "who were they?" "Well, there were hundreds of spirits hanging around that place, man, so many it was like an old zombie movie, or a battlefield or something, spirits everywhere."

"There was this one guy, Bubba Johnson, he said he drove a city transit bus for twenty five years on the that route. He also, lived there in Claremont when he was alive," says Bob, "and he knew of that guy in Unit # 58 named Frank Kirby. Said that he never left his house, they say in 40 years!" "Bubba Johnson huh, are you pulling my leg, man?" I asked. "Yeah, dude, that was his name. I mean, why would he bullshit me?" Bob says. "Alright his name was Bubba Johnson. Dude, I'm sorry, it just struck me as funny. I'm sorry, go on with the story," I said. "Alright then, there was another guy I stopped to talk to as well," said Bob, "who called himself Marty, just Marty. He said he lived in Claremont while he was alive, too, and also knew of the weirdo in Unit # 58."

"This Marty guy lived with his mother all his life until the age of forty. He told me that his mother had a heart attack and died while at work at the bucket factory." "A bucket factory, you say?" I asked. "Yes, that's what he said, now let me finish. When she didn't come home after a couple of days to make his meals, old Marty stuck his head in the oven and turned on the gas."

"That wouldn't work, would it?" I asked. "I guess it did," Bob said, "he told me, he fell asleep on the floor with the gas turned on with his head laying on the open oven door." "Wow, I guess in that case it would then, huh? so then what happened?" I asked.

"Well, both Bubba and Marty told me about the little girl that went missing in '61, her name was Ellen O'Grady," said Bob. "She was your sister Linda's age at the time she went missing. That night, she had on an "Olive Oyl" Halloween costume and her older brother was dressed as Popeye." "What happened?" I asked. "Bubba said, he overheard all the kids on the bus talking the day after Halloween, say that when the Orange Man came out of the woods all the kids scattered but little Ellen just stood there, to scared to move.

The Orange Man, stopped for a moment and stared down at her, then he just picked her up, ran into the woods, and was gone."

"Bubba, told me that he would never let his little kids go trick or treating by themselves, but only with him, or with the big kid next door. Marty chimed in that was just the way it was back then, it was no big deal to see kids seven or eight years old walking alone or riding their bikes all over town."

"Bob, I'm going to drop off Chrystal and the Peanut at my sister's house this morning so they can go shopping downtown. What say you and I go to Claremont?" I said. "Sounds like a plan," replies Bob.

On my way across town to Claremont we went by my old junior high school and the neighborhood we moved to after leaving the Projects. Boy, how freaking sad is this, I thought to myself. I almost thought I was in a third world country and I for damn sure don't want to break down here, even with AAA. As we pull down the main road Bobby comments how different it looks in the daylight. Hmm, I wondered where the big renovation happened. The place still looks the same, maybe some new street lights and landscaping on the outside, must have been an interior remodel, I guess. "Let's park and walk down to the ball field, Bob," I said.

When we get to the bottom of the path it opened out onto a large playing field where a bunch of young people are playing all kinds of sports from baseball to soccer, with a few hippie types throwing a frisbee around. "I think I'll take a break on those benches over there, Bob, you go ahead and wander around if you like," I said. Bob just nods and disappears from view.

After just a short time I hear, a soft voice say, "are you Mr. Rick?" As I turn around there stands a cute little spirit, just as faint as my Mother must appear to Bobby, only I can see this little one standing right in front of me.

She has strawberry blond hair with a mask on top of her head and what could be somewhat of a glow all around her and getting brighter. I knew straight away who this must be. "Hello, Sweetheart, is your name Ellen?" she shakes her head up and down and says, "ah hah."

"Your friend Mr. Bob, told me to come over and say hello," said little Ellen. "Sweetheart, why are you still here in this place?" I asked her. "The bad men in orange wouldn't let me leave," she cried. I can't help but think that Frank Kirby, passed away not too long ago, and she said, (bad men?) "Bobby, where are you? I need you," I say in my head as not to scare off little Ellen. Just as soon as I thought it, Bobby was there. "Sorry it took me so long, Rick," says Bob, panting like he just ran the four minute mile. "I was busy kicking some orange man butt." "Couldn't have been to hard," I said, "wasn't he an old man?" "Well, your partly right," replied Bob "that was the son." "Say what?" I said. "No, really, I did not expect what happened, that's for damn sure," replied Bob. "I found what must have been the stupid assholes hot spot where he would sit and inspect all his ill gotten booty from all those poor kids through the years," said Bob. "Hot spot huh, what do you mean?" I asked.

"Yeah, the memories still lingered in the air of what he would do there, he would sit on this big chunk of concrete, (left over from when they built the little league dugouts) and gorge himself on candy and laugh at how he would scare the kids each year and get away with it. It's also where he carried little Ellen off to. And, when her parents, friends and neighbors were out looking for her, yelling out her name, it's where that orange fucker hid and held his filthy hand over her mouth and nose to quiet her from calling out. It's also behind that big chunk of concrete, is where the orange freak buried her."

"So Bob, I'm confused," I said, "you said that was the son." "Yeah, it was," Bob explained, "when I found the little girl peaking out from behind a tree, I coaxed her out, she told me to be careful, there were bad men here. I looked around and I saw only the one old orange bastard coming at me with his hands clenched, so I quickly told Ellen to run over across the field to the man with the nice face called Mr. Rick. Then, I knocked the old bastard down and was about to send him to hell." "You can do that?" I asked. "Something inside of me told me I could Rick, I didn't know for sure if I could, I only knew I had to try. So anyway, as I'm strangling this old fart another pair of orange hands grabs me around the neck."

"What the Hell?" I asked. "Yeah, what the hell is right, so I banged the old boy's head on the ground and he vanished. Now my hands are free to deal with the one on my back. Who the hell are you I asked as I was throwing him to the ground," said Bob.

"That was my boy, Frank Jr. and now, you've ruined everything," he cried out. "This 'new' orange prick, was maybe mid to late thirty's, so he put up more of a fight, and man, he sure as hell tried. I wondered what he was talking about, because he was half the age of that ass hole I just sent to hell? As we were squaring off he told me before he passed on, he, left his boy well taken care of so he'd never have to go out into the world so full of leaches and harlots. He was a fucking loon, Rick," Bob explained.

"When my Frank Jr. found my orange outfit hidden in the closet, I was hoping one day he would put it on and carry on where I left off." The loony bastard, went on to say. "Is that right, you sick bastard," I said, "I'm sorry about that but it's time you joined your boy. Then I, beat that vile mother fucker with my bare hands, showing him no mercy. Rick, something weird happened while I was standing over him." "What was that buddy?" I asked. "Well, I reached down and grabbed his head in my hands and squeezed it till his head crumbled like an ash off a cigarette." "Whoa, Bob, that was surely the power of God working through you man," I said. "I think so Rick." "Oh man, you had direct contact with pure evil, my friend. And it sounds like you sent them both straight to hell where they belonged." I said. "I think your right Rick, at least I hope so," Bob replied.

Bobby, calms down, then motions to little Ellen, who's been standing there this whole time, hiding behind her mask. He picks her up and holds Ellen on his lap, takes her mask off and gives her the longest hug, something this precious little girl has needed for too long. He tilts his hat back and holds her little chin in his hand and tells her it's alright, you can go home now. Bobby strokes her cheek with the back of his fingers and tells her, your Mommy and Daddy have been looking for you, and they're waiting for you. As she smiles back at my friend, I can see she's missing her two front teeth and I can't help but laugh and cry at the same time. She climbs off of Bobby's knee and starts to walk away. "Goodbye Ellen," I say. She waves to me and says, "goodbye, Mr. Rick."

As she slowly walks away she stops, turns around and runs back to Bobby. Bobby, drops to one knee and catches her in his arms, then that little cutie says, "thank you, Mr. Bob, I love you." Bob smiles, nods his head and tells Ellen, he loves her too, then she vanishes.

"Good job Bob," I said, "I think I know now why the Good Lord has decided to leave you here for awhile, my friend."

"And if I can add to that," I said "maybe it was in his plan that we hook up again." "You think?" Bob, said. "I think so pal," I replied. "Hey Rick, lets make like sheep herder's and get the flock outta here and go back to your sister's house to see what treasures they found today." "Sounds good pal, now that little Ellen is on her way to Heaven where she belongs and justice has been served with a side order of Bobby, I'm feeling good again. "How about we do a little site seeing the rest of the week?" I ask Bob. "Okay, Lets go." Bob agrees.

CHAPTER 7.

Trip to Vegas

Part 1. Eddie

After a wonderful visit with my sister and her family it's time now to head back to California. I don't think I'll ever forget this visit for several reasons; first and foremost I had a great time showing my granddaughter where I came from, plus being able to show her a little bit of our Country's heritage in Washington, D.C. was great, too. It was pretty cool to see those little nine year old eyes go all a gaga a couple of times, and yet bored to tears at others. I remember coming here as a small boy myself.

Of course my lovely wife has been back here with me many times in the past thirty five years and has seen much of D.C., Maryland and Pennsylvania. I don't think, as an American, you can ever get tired of it. I know I don't, nor does Chrystal. My little one will have a few good stories to tell when she gets back to school. I think everyone should bring their children to Washington D.C. at least once in their life, but as long as Vegas, Disneyland and Hawaii look like more fun it'll never be at the top of the vacation list.

Hmmm, maybe the Smithsonian Institute should put in a water park with a few cool rides. Oh well, where would they put it, anyway. And, of course, just as important was Bobby and I being able to help little Ellen find her way to Heaven, I'm certain that's where that precious little child is right now. And what can I say about Bobby, that cold plate of justice he dealt to those looney orange bastards would have made Dirty Harry proud.

I'm still a little puzzled, as anyone would be, to have this gift. Being able to see and hear the dead. At times it's almost like having a curse, if there is such a thing as a curse, but at other times, some of the nice folks we've met and have been able to help, have left me with really fond and loving memories. Then, I feel truly blessed to have this gift. Although it sometimes gets real overwhelming, I do hope Bobby stays around for a long time. Hell, I think in some ways we're better friends now than when he was alive, if only I could share our adventure's with Chrystal. Maybe one day, but not yet.

After being home a couple of days I get a call from my old friend Chet, who's been trying to track down his brother's kid with not much luck, and needs my help. The boys name is Eddie and is nineteen or twenty. I guess Eddie hasn't checked in with his mom or dad in over a week now, and they're awfully worried. I met him once at a party at Chet's house. He was kind of a little punk if I remember right. My old friend Chet made millions during the 80's when the dot com craze was new, and unlike some folks that come into a fortune, Chet never changed a bit.

We still play golf occasionally and meet for a drink whenever both of us are in town. Chet and his brother, Charlie, used to frame houses with me when we were young carpenters; Chet was a real sharp and talented builder, along with being a stand up guy. On the other hand brother Charlie, or "Racecar" as we sometimes called him, was just the opposite, Charlie was a real rascal.

Brother Charlie got his nickname because of an old piece of crap '68 Chevelle he use to drive with an old worn out 396 motor. That car could have been a sweet ride had he only put a few dollars into it, but Charlie only cared about partying with the ladies and getting high on the weekend. So the poor Chevelle got all rusty and worn out, kinda like that pretty girl in the neighborhood we all knew that hit the booze and pasta a little too hard. I think most neighborhoods got a gal like this, I know we did.

So, anyway, Chet helped Charlie all through the years as most brothers would. Sure enough, Charlie finally did grow up and take responsibility for his actions, but boy was he a late bloomer. Whenever I see him now with Chet I can't help but to rag on him about, shit where do I begin? How long he wore that mullet, those balloon pants, the high top Converse sneakers, and, oh yeah, holding on to that 8 track tape player just a little too long. He said he wanted to keep the car original, yeah right. Charlie finally buckled down and cut his hair, and cleaned up his act when he was maybe thirty two, after he saw the world passing him by. He parked that Chevelle in his Mom's back yard and took a job with a company Chet set up to handle all the properties he had been buying though the years; he was doing great. Charlie got married, had a son and named him Eddie, after Eddie Van Halen, of course, and like his brother, is now a friend I'm proud to know.

Chet, asked me to find his brother's boy, he told me; do what you have to do, whatever it takes. Eddie is a musician and plays guitar, pretty good too, I hear. Chet, said he left home a month ago to go to Vegas to play with a band who saw his video he posted on You Tube and they hired him to play a gig there. It's been 10 days now with no contact from Eddie, and Charlie and his wife are freaking out. I'll get all the needed info and a current picture of Eddie, then I guess I'll pack up for a trip to Las Vegas.

"Hey, Bobby, you out there buddy?" "Yeah, I'm here Rick, what's up?" Bob replies. "Bob, I'm pulling the Buick out and heading to Vegas, you want to come with?" I ask. "Sure," he replies, "by the time you get to Reno don't be surprised when I'm sitting in the back seat," he says.

Chrystal, asked if she moves some plans around can she join me for a few days. "Well, of course" I said. What man in his right mind would say no if his wife wanted to go with him to Vegas? Not a happy, healthy, smart man, I can tell you that! Truth is, I enjoy her company."

"By the time we get up Highway 80 into Reno, I look in the rearview mirror and true to his word there sat Bobby, with both arms stretched out across the back of the seat just chilling out. I think to myself, glad you could join us, my friend. Bob, sends back his thought to me, glad to be here, dude, let's roll.

As we travel down Highway 95 through Nevada in our bitchin '57 Buick Road Master I can't believe how much I'm really enjoying this ride, I mean Highway 95 from Carson City to Las Vegas is not the most scenic stretch of road in America, but I could ride in this car all day with it's sweet interior and it's big block power. Of course, there's the occasional stop at the tourist traps along the way where Chrystal always seems to find something. So, feeling a little hungry we stop at a roadside restaurant just outside of Hawthorne. I say to Chrystal, "this must be a good place, there's a half a dozen big rigs in the parking lot and the truckers always know the best places to eat." I turn and look at the back seat to see if Bob approves and he just gives me that "are you kidding me" look, shakes his head, then smiles.

While inside my wife comments on how clean and nice it is, "yeah it is huh, babe," I replied. Sitting behind us was a nice looking older gal who I assumed was a trucker, she smiled and said hello. After we ordered we started up a conversation with her, and I noticed she wore a POW*MIA pin on her vest, along with a 30 year service pin from the trucking company she hauled for.

"You folks driving that beautiful old Buick out there?" she asked. "Yes Ma'am," I replied. "Oh please, don't call me Ma'am" she says, "my name's Mary Jane, but my friends call me Mom." "And I'll bet you got a lot of friends after driving for all those years," I said. "Hmm, oh the pin," she says. "I guess I've met a few nice folks along the way, and some not so nice, ones, too, in all the years I've been driving." She looks out into the parking lot and gestures to one of the cleanest Freightliners I've ever seen. "I gotta tell ya, Mary Jane, I don't think I've ever seen a lavender big rig before," I said, as Chrystal adds, "I think it's lovely." "Thank you, my dears," she replies.

Mary Jane, looked a whole hell of a lot like the actress, Kathy Bates, with shoulder length gray hair and very little make up. There was also a very sweet southern draw in her voice. While eating our meal we had a real nice visit with her. Hell, we stayed and told stories for an hour, over coffee. "So, may I ask about the POW*MIA pin, Mary Jane?" "Sure darlin," she replies, "I wear that to honor my husband Joe who went to Vietnam in '68 with the army." Bobby, who's been sitting at the lunch counter all this time leans in to hear the story about her husband, as he was there in '68 as well.

"My Joe, went missing in action only three months into his tour of duty, we had only been married for a year." "Just a year?" I asked. "Yes, but I think we must have fell in love when we were both five or six years old back in Greenville, South Carolina." "And never a word on what happened?" I asked. "No, sugar, they just speculated but never really knew, that's war," she said. "And you never married again or had any children?" I asked. "Oh, heavens no," she replied, "Joey, was the love of my life."

∽

"Well shut my mouth, will you look at the time!" says our new friend. "I've got to get rollin, it was a pleasure chatting with you two." Mary Jane, extends her hand to Chrystal and then pulls her in for a goodbye hug, then she turns to me and gives me a hug as well. "Goodbye, sweet lady," I say, "it certainly has been a pleasure talking with you, too." As she turns to walk away she says, "and remember, the next time we meet, please call me Mom." "We better get back on the road, too Honey," I said. Bob nods his head and is gone. "What a wonderful lady Mary Jane was," my wife says. "Hmm, I agree I liked her a lot," I reply. As we pull back on Highway 95 I notice Bobby is nowhere in site, I think to myself, I'll give him some space and not bother him for a while.

We drive for a few more hours and pull into Tonopah. It's getting dark and I'm not much in the mood for traveling at night. Chrystal's sound asleep so I pull into the Best Western right on the frontage road, get us a room and put my wife to bed. I find a liquor store and get myself a little bottle of tequila and a bottle of diet Pepsi, I had some thinking to do and a cocktail and cigar was just the ticket.

Sitting by the pool with the door to our room in site, I enjoy my cigar and drink and again wondered where Bob has gone off too. As quick as that he was sitting in the chair next to me. "Hey Bob, where you been?" I asked. "Well Rick, I was curious so I went to find out what happened to Mary Jane's husband, Joe," replied Bob. "How so," I asked, "I mean, you don't know her do you?" "No," says Bob, "but her full name was on the cab of the truck and I've been to Vietnam, so it wasn't as hard as you think." "Cool, what did you find out buddy?" I asked.

"Well," said Bob, "back in '68 her husband's unit was in the Central Highlands area of Vietnam which is where I found him." "You did find him, and he of course was, dead?" I asked. "Of course," Bob said. "But why has he been over there all this time, why did he never come home with the others? Oh shit, I just answered my own question," I said. "It's because he was never found, is that right Bob?" "That's correct my friend, but that's all changed now that I found him." "Oh?" I said. "Yeah, after I got him away from the spot where he was killed, I spent some time with him. Rick, I tried to school him on how to shake off all the bullshit he experienced over there, as I did. It's not easy but you can do it. I also tried to teach him the little bit I know about the time and space difference between, the living and spirit world. Then I simply told him to go and clean himself up and get his ass back home where he can be with, and watch over his, Mary Jane. It's been a lot longer than you think," I told him.

"I showed him what I could, told him about what he could expect and to not be sad, but to learn all he could from this place, and that there's a much better place waiting for him. I also told him about Mary Jane and how she never remarried, and how she thinks of him everyday and yearns for the time when they can be together again."

"Wow Bob, you could have been a priest," I said. "Just doing what I can man, too much sadness in the world, don't you think, Rick?" "I do, pal," I replied. As I snuff out my cigar and walk towards my room I tell him, "that's why you're my hero, Bob, good night, buddy."

After breakfast we're back on the road. Chrystal, says we'll probably be in Vegas by late afternoon the way this Buick runs. "You got that right, babe, I don't think I've ever been so happy with a vehicle in my life, as I am with this beauty. I get as excited as a fat kid with a birthday cake every time I get in it. I just love this big ole piece of American iron," I said. "Me, too," replies Chrystal. "It still blows my mind that the Mingus family gave you this as a gift for helping them." "Still blows my mind too, sweetie, like you'll never know," I say. "Yeah, me too," said Bobby. "You know, if I was still alive I would treat this car like the beautiful women she is," adds Bob. "It is a dream machine, ain't it Bob," I reply. "It's a groovy ride alright," says Bob. "What are you smiling about, babe?" my wife asked. "Just the car, sweetie, just the car," I said.

As we cruise along I say in my head, Bob, this kid Eddie shouldn't be too hard to find should he? "Nah, I don't think so Rick," replies Bob, "I've already got a few leads on him and will probably know where he is in a little while, the cosmic grapevine you know." "But of course," I say, "and just what kind of leads do you have, if you don't mind me asking?" "Dead musicians that came to Vegas to play gigs mostly, plus a few young groupies and nightlife people who I saw hanging out at clubs and casinos. There's been a shady side to the music scene in that lovely town for decades," says Bob. "As a matter of fact, I'm going back again now to follow up on something, I'll be back later. See ya."

～

We pull up to the valet parking at the MGM and right away a small crowd of people gather around my Buick.

I look up at the marquee and notice that the Vegas Music Awards is happening this week and I wonder if maybe they think I'm somebody special. After the valet grabs our bags and compliments the car, the star gazers realize I'm a nobody and wander off. I think to myself, I sure as hell am a somebody, to my lovely wife and family and maybe a few friends, and that's something. It's all I really give a shit about.

Now if this was a custom car show I'd be a somebody, alright, I'd be the guy who owed the most bitchin '57 Buick Road Master in the show, no, on the planet! Ha, take that you music snobs, and ha again!

～

Bobby, shows up in the elevator just as we're heading down to the restaurant to grab a bite to eat and tells me that he has news, and it's not good. "Honey, I really have to make a few calls and check out a few leads, you don't mind do you? After all, that is why I'm here," I say to Chrystal. "Not a problem hon. Keep your phone on in case I need you," she replies. "I think I'll take this opportunity to look up a few old friends from my school days, after all I did grow up here. See you later, and be safe," she says. "Okay, Bob, whatcha got, man?" "Well, Rick, the word is he got mixed up with the wrong people, and must have done or said the wrong thing. They say he probably wound up in the desert." "Shit man, that is not what I wanted to hear. Okay let's go find our boy."

The desert around Las Vegas covers an extremely large area of land, most of it is government owned land but a lot of private land as well. "I'm going to have to rent a four wheel drive for sure," I said. "Yeah, I know," says Bob. "it's pretty rough out there, too. After I got back from overseas I took a job installing radio towers and we put a few of them up here." "I remember you telling me about that job," I said. "Well, we'll be alright." "There's no "we" Rick," says Bob, "there's only you, I'm dead remember. Not to worry though my friend, I got your back." "I know you do, pal, I always know that," I replied.

It didn't take long for Bob, to leave and then get back with more info from the local dead music scene. As I'm driving out to the Red Rock Canyon area outside of town my buddy appears in the passenger seat beside me in my rental Jeep. "I never liked these," Bob, says. "Me neither," I said, "they don't have enough power and they're uncomfortable for big guys, but it's all they had. What's up?" "Okay, here's the low down on what happened to our boy. I guess Charlie's son Eddie had a little secret that he hid from his family," said Bob. "Oh," I replied.

"It seems as though Eddie was one of many small time drug dealers in Sacramento working for a large gang down south, and he somehow pissed these guys off," added Bob. "Let me guess," I said, "they lured him down here with the ruse of it being some kind of break in the music business, huh?" "You pretty much nailed it my friend, the story is he was a little light with his receipts one too many times and they had to teach him a lesson, plus send a message." "Same old story, huh buddy," I said, "young and stupid, especially when drugs are involved. Damn it, Eddie, you stupid shit, this is not going to end well, I can see it now." "You know a wise man once said, stupid is as stupid does," says Bob.

"They told him he was going to play a gig here and if they liked him he would then be invited to join the band back in LA for a recording session," Bob explained. "So, what happened to our boy?" I ask. "Well, you're driving in the right direction, Rick, keep going this way," replies Bob, "I'll know it when we get there."

"So, you say he's out here somewhere Bob." "Yeah, Rick, the Kat I talked to said he was in a cave about a half mile north of mile marker 26, just off the canyon road." Hmmm, this is really going to suck, I thought.

As we reach the area, I park the Jeep and then we make our way up to the canyon wall where I can see a cave. "Damn, Bob, if he's in there they wanted him to be found, cause there's got to be hikers and mountain bikers galore that go through here all the time," I said. "Exactly," replies Bob. " Ah shit, it's starting to rain, Bob," I say. "Really," says Bob, "what do you want, an umbrella, maybe some rubber boots?" "Yes, please," I replied. As we enter the cave I notice it gets more narrow and the ceiling gets lower the further I go in, and I say to Bob, "would you mind going ahead to check it out cause I'm not too found of this kind of thing and I don't know how much further I can go?" "Sure buddy, I'll be right back," Bob replies.

There's graffiti all over the walls, and I think to myself if I'm not mistaking these must be Mexican gang signs. Bob, returns and tells me that Eddie is just a little further inside the cave. "Yes, I heard you," he says, "they are Mexican gang signs." "It sounds like it's raining even harder now, damn it."

After getting on my hands and knees and crawling for thirty to forty feet the cave opened up to a room where I can stand again. Sure enough, there lies Eddie leaning up against a wall wearing only his Calvin Klien's, and he's, "ah, shit man, is that what I think it is Bob?" I ask. "It sure is Rick, those Mexican bastards wrapped him up from head to toe with barb wire," said Bob. "Not only him but look, his guitar over there is also wrapped in barb wire," "WTF," I said.

"That's also a message," said Bob," the message is if you fuck with us we'll not only kill you but kill the thing you love the most as well." "I guess it's a good thing our boy didn't bring a girlfriend along huh, Bob? those sick bastards?" I add. "Yeah man, sick," answers Bob.

Just then I noticed the water coming in the cave, and it was coming in so fucking quick I was getting a little more than worried. Plus, to make matters worse all the desert creatures must use this cave for shelter as well, because the frogs and snakes were coming in by the dozens! "Damn it, Bob, I'm freaking out here, what am I going to do?" "Stop, and calm down Rick, the snakes and other critters just want to get out of the rain, too." "Be still, and let them pass by, they're on there way to the back of the cave," Bob explained. "OoooKay, I'll try," I said. To my surprise Bob was right, they all just swam by me like I wasn't even there.

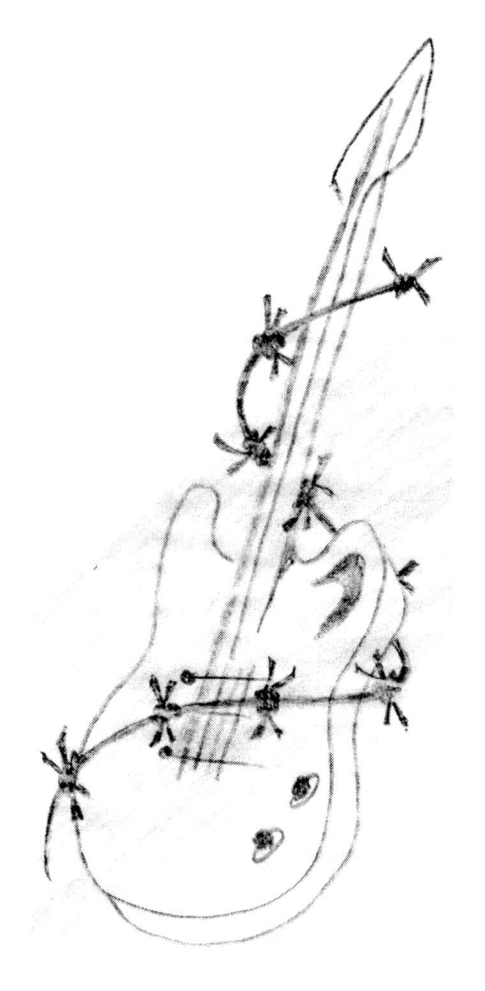

"So Bob, where is Eddie's spirit now?" I asked. "Eddie's spirit, is at the back of the cave," Bob, explained, "I guess he was overdosed with a big bag of heroin so, the dumb shit thinks he's still to stoned to move, and I also think he's afraid of the dark." "You mean he doesn't know that he's dead?" I ask. "Seems that way," replied Bob.

As the rainstorm lets up the water in the cave stills, then starts to recede a little. "You alright buddy?" asked Bob. "Yes, much better now that the rain has stopped, thanks man," I said. "Well, what are you going to do about Eddie?" Bob asked. "First of all, let me get out of this God forsaken cave then I'll call an old friend of my wife's who's on the Sherriff's department to come and get the body, then, I'll have to call Chet." "Chet, can tell his brother, damn it, I hate this shit," I said.

"Sorry about your friend's son," says Bob. "Yeah, thanks buddy, not to sound too callous but, you know what they say, that's why they call it dope. So where is his spirit now Bob?" I asked. "He's still at the back of the cave, Rick, and if it's alright with you I'm going to fucking leave him there," replies Bob. "With my blessings, brother, that little asshole had everything going for him," I said. "He had a well "to do" loving family and every opportunity under the sun to make something of himself, but no, he'd rather get high and deal drugs? There will be no sympathy from me, pal, fuck him. Let him rot there in that cave for all eternity, let's go." "My feelings exactly, Rick," says Bob.

After Chet flew in to have the boy picked up and flown back to Sacramento, he thanks me and asked me for my bill. "No charge, Chet," I told him. "Rick, please let me pay you," replies Chet, had you not done this for me, who knows how long it would be until we knew what happened to Eddie." As he starts to write out a check I leaned forward to see the amount - $10,000, I tell him to just give me $1,000 to cover my gas and Hotel and give the rest to the Sacramento Homeless Shelter. Chet smiles, hands me my check and says thanks again, my friend and please, give Chrystal my love.

"Well honey, are you ready for a groovy ride back home? How about we head over to LA and up the coast," I ask. "No Sweetie, I'd like to go back the way we came, if you don't mind," replies Chrystal. "How about you Bob?" I ask in my thoughts. "You know Rick, I think I'll take the plane, the "Astral Plane" that is," replies Bobby, "ha ha… nah, really I'll see you on the road."

Trip to Vegas

Part 2. Mary Jane

"**M**an I'll be happy when this town is no longer in my rear view mirror, huh, Honey?" "I don't know why you hate it here so much Rick, after all, we did meet here and Danielle was born here," Chrystal replies. "Oh, it's just too hot I guess," I tell her, God forbid I had to explain what really happened here. "I'm sorry about Charlie's son Eddie, too babe. When we get home I'll send the family some nice flowers," says Chrystal." "Thanks, Hon."

As we cruise up the highway cars, trucks and motorcycles are zooming by like we're sitting still and I've got the cruise control set at 78 mph. It's a good thing they don't want to race because I'd show 'em what this 502 big block can do, ha. The old hot rod boys know, and give you respect when you pass by with your throaty rumble, again I say to myself, ha. "Alright Ricky," says Chrystal, "I know that look and you're NOT going to race these kids. Take it to the drag strip, but not with me in it, please." "Ricky?" says Bob. "Dude, you're back." "Hey, only my Mother and Chrystal ever call me that, usually when they're pissed," I replied. "Okay, Ricky." "Come on Boo Boo, don't you start with me," I add. "Ouch, you got me with the Boo Boo," said Bob.

"Man, there are a shit load of teenagers on the road today aren't there? Oh, you know what, they just graduated a few days ago, didn't they?" asked Bob. "Yeah, that must be it," I said. "You know what babe, I think these kids must have just graduated, what do you think?" asked Chrystal. "Yeah, I think you're right Hon," I reply.

"You know what, how about we stop at the next motor lodge we see with a bar/restaurant attached and relax the rest of the evening? Hell, we've been on the road now, five hours?" "What an old fart you've turned into," says Bob. "I know huh. Well, truth is I'd love a freaking ice cold beer and a cigar about now and I can't do that in my new car now, can I?" I said.

"Oh, look, honey, that looks like a nice one," says Chrystal. "Oh, look, 'honey' and it has a casino attached, Ricky," adds Bob. "That's enough out of you young man, don't make me come back there," I replied. "Good one buddy," says Bob, "hey, I'll see you later man, I need to check on a few things."

As we pull in I recognize the lavender Freightliner in the side parking lot straight away, it's our new friend Mary Jane's rig. "Look over there, babe, isn't that our friend Mary Jane's truck and trailer?" I ask. "It must be. Darn it, I hope she's around, I'd love to see her again," replies Chrystal. I go get us a nice room and we head off to the casino.

Chrystal's, having a good time playing the slots and hit's a quarter machine for two hundred and fifty dollars and thinks she's queen for a day. I hope she knows she's my queen everyday. She'll probably give it all back to another machine before we leave, anyway. "Having fun, are you Hon," I shout across the room, over the casino noise and music coming from the lounge act in the corner.

And wouldn't you know it they're playing, you guessed it "Reelin in the years… stowing away the time." Chrystal, gives me the Queens wave and a smile, and gets back to hitting the buttons. I look over at Bob, now busy looking over the Pit bosses shoulder, and shake my head, he gives me that look this time with a wink and then wanders off. How's does he do that, I wonder? Oh well, I guess it is his favorite song.

I know this place is old but it sure looks nice, I wonder what went on here in its heyday. "Hi Rick, I'm back." "Oh, where are you Bob?" I ask. "Just over here behind the cute little 21 dealer, I'm watching the old pit boss with the bad hair piece play "hide the paycheck," in the back pockets of her Wranglers," says Bob. "Brushing off the lint is he?" I ask. "Ah huh," replies Bob, "I'll bet before the night's out this old boy's going to be playing hide the something else, if you know what I mean," says Bob. "Must be a drag working in this boring place way the hell down the road from Vegas," I add. "It wasn't always that way, Rick." "The hell you say, tell me more, my brother," I say in my best 'hillbilly' voice. "Hmm, maybe that cute little dealer would rather have you brushing the lint off her 'J Lo' hump, ya think?" says Bob. "I don't think so buddy, not this cowboy, I'm a happily married man, you know," I reply.

"You know, Rick, I'm really glad we can communicate telepathically now because, as I've said before, you sure would look like a fool walking around talking to yourself," says Bob. "You mean like all those people with that hands free ear piece phones talking away as they're shopping or pumping gas, you mean like those fucking rude assholes," I replied. "Hey dude, you got a real problem with those people don't you?" Bob says.

"Rick, you know that old expression "if these walls could talk," well, they're talking to me right now. There's a lot that's gone on at this place through the years. I can almost see it, and feel it. It's like when you fast forward a show you've recorded, only faster, but pausing every now and then at the good stuff," says Bob. "Wow, you mean you can see what went on here in the past?" I ask. "Not really," says Bob. "Shit, if that were the case this realm would surely be Looneyville you know. And don't call me Shirley. It just started happening back in Baltimore, remember I told you about the place where that crazy orange bastard would eat his candy? That was the first time." "And since then?" I ask." "Not really," replies Bob, "because unless it really grabs my attention I can ignore it." "What do you mean, grabs your attention?" I ask.

"Have you ever walked into somebody's house and their Grandma from the old country is cooking something in the kitchen that reeks to high heaven?" says Bob. "And makes your eyes water so bad you have to excuse yourself to get outside for some fresh air," I add. "Yeah, ha ha, like that," says Bob. "Well, when it slaps me in the face and grabs my attention like that, I stop and take notice to what I'm being shown."

"You mean it stinks?" I ask. "No, damn it Rick, I can't smell anything in here, I just used that as a metaphor because at those times I'm talking about, it's just so thick and troublesome I have to stop and see what the trouble is or was, to be correct. I'm only now getting a handle on it, you know how I go off from time to time." "Yeah, where do you go?" I ask. "It doesn't matter where I go buddy," replies Bob, "there's hardly a place on earth that something hasn't happened." "Hmm, I guess that right there is a testament to man's greed and lust, huh Bob?" I ask. "Yeah, I guess you could put it that way, but getting back to this place, I get the vibe this place was a mecca for young performers from Vegas to Hollywood. Movie stars and singers came here with their agents and producers including a few mob types all through the 40's, 50's and 60's" said Bob. "But why way out here?" I ask. "And what did they do here?"

"A lot of pretty weird and kinky stuff went on here, Rick," replies Bob. "They started coming out here as an extension to the casting couch, you know what I mean. Way out here, they got away from the press, husbands and wives, plus the fans. The agents and producers could have their way with the young stars and starlets." "You get all that from just, what, scanning the room?" I ask. "And especially the motor lodge," replies Bob. "I can tell you this buddy, there's been so much kinky, sick, fucking shit that's gone on here with so many stars you wouldn't believe it. I don't want to pop your bubble so don't ask me who they were." "Okay, I won't, but I gotta know," I said. "Was Marilyn Monroe ever here?"

"What did I just ask you Rick, and yes, she was often a guest in bungalow #12. Now stop, don't ask anymore." "Oh, alright, how about Frank Sinatra? Was he ever here?" I ask. "Oh, yeah, ole blue eyes liked bungalow #12 too. Now that's it, really. If I told you everything I know you could write a book. And that wouldn't be fair to their families and fans now, would it?" says Bob. "Ahh, screw it, I'll tell you later."

"Chrystal, seems to be having a good time," says Bob. "Yeah, she's not a real gambler but she loves to get out and go on trips, as you know," I say.

"I know, I remember, she loves to travel Rick," said Bob. "Honey, isn't that our new friend Mary Jane over there having dinner all alone?" asks my wife. "Sure looks like it," I replied. "Why don't you go over and say hello, and ask her to join us." "I think I will," says Chrystal.

"Bob, I better join Chrystal over there for a bit," I say. "Go ahead pal," Bob replies, "I'll be close if you need me." "Hello Mary Jane, how've you been dear?" I ask. "Oh, hello sugar," she says as she reaches over to kiss my cheek. "Please, come sit down and join me." "Where've you been since the last time we've seen you Mary Jane?" I ask.

"Well, I've dropped a load in LA and picked up another in Bakersfield. Now I'm on my way up to Carson City to drop this trailer full of electronics off to a Best Buy store and then, I may just take a little time to myself, Hon," says Mary Jane. "I've been doing this for too long now, and I'm thinking maybe it's time for me to sell my rig and take up gardening like a real southern lady," she adds. "Well, the best of luck to you in whatever you do dear lady," I tell her.

My thoughts go to Bob, "Hey, Bob, whatever happened to her husband Joe? Did he ever get out of the jungle and come back home to the US?" "Yeah, he's here Rick, he's across the room by the nickel slots in the corner, but he's afraid to approach his Mary Jane. I guess because of all the time that's gone by," says Bob. "Hmm, I don't know buddy, this is no time to act like a skittish school boy asking the cute girl in class out for a date. Now's the time to man up and watch over your gal." "I think so too, Rick, but dig it, I'm not one to give this fella advise after all he's been through," replies Bob. "I mean, think about how he must feel man, he was killed and left in the jungle for well over forty years." "I guess he has every right to be angry," I reply, as I nod to the waitress and hold up my cup for a refill.

"Yeah, he's a little angry, but not so much with the war but with himself for missing out on a lifetime with his Mary Jane." "Hmm, I can only imagine what he must be feeling," I said. My attention turns back to Mary Jane, as I can see she's getting ready to leave, and I want to say goodbye. "Goodbye, sweet lady, I really hope we meet again one day," I hand her one of my cards and tell her if she's ever in northern California to please give us a call and stop by. "I surely will sugar," she replies, as she hugs me like a Mother would hug her children, it made me think of my mom for a moment. As I hug her back I'm smitten by her scent, it's a mixture of lavender and Jack Daniels is the best I can describe. She gets up on her tip toes and plants a big kiss on my cheek, leaving a big perfect red tattoo of her lips on my face. It was hours until I notice it in the rear view mirror. It made me smile to remember her…

As we peel out of the parking lot and put this this little Nevada town behind us, Bobby informs me that Mary Jane's husband, Joe, is sitting in the cab of her truck with her. "That's a good start, huh Bob, that's right where he needs to be for the healing to begin."

～

It didn't take too long while driving down the road to get a little annoyed with the amount of teenagers on the road. "Man, where in the hell did these kids learn to drive anyway, at the amusement park? I mean, I like to hot rod as much as the next guy, but come on, this is crazy town!" "I guess there isn't much else for kids to do in the Nevada boonies other than drink a little and race, up and down the highway," says Bob. "What, they never heard of a good game of "Twister" or Spin the Bottle?" I reply. Bobby just shakes his head and laughs, then tells me to hurry up and get past the outskirts of this bullshit little town and maybe the road will calm down.

After a mile or so I say to my wife, "Honey, look, isn't that Mary Jane's big rig up there?" Crystal adds, "Looks like it babe." Bobby, says, "I gotta funny feeling about this day Rick, something bad is about to happen and there's nothing you or I can do to stop it. So just keep your speed down and really pay attention, Okay man," says Bob. "Maybe, just maybe, we can be of some help." "Shit, Bob, this is like watching a movie man, you know something is going to happen but you don't know what. WTH, are you sure of this or are you just having a premonition, buddy?" "I'm certain of one thing, Rick, something's going to happen. I don't know what or when but soon, I just fucking know it."

～

Looks like the same bunch of kids racing up and down this stretch of road for the last hour. A pretty nice looking white early 70's Ford 4WD with a couple of kids in the back holding on to a chrome roll bar. And, a little red Toyota 4WD with a couple of kids, plus a lowered Honda Civic full of teenage girls and another little foreign piece of shit also full of teenage girls. And finally, believe it or not, a sweet, green '62 Pontiac Bonneville. The Pontiac has tinted windows so I can't really see who is in it, but they're being cool, unlike the others. It's that little Honda and its sister piece of crap foreign car with those damn silly girls. What's up with young girls anyway? Drinking and throwing the beer cans out the window. I mean shit, on top of their Highway shenanigans, they're littering, too. You can bet your ass their parents wouldn't dig it if they knew how they were celebrating graduation. But, maybe that's how they do it here, in this town.

Bobby, tells me to be alert, it's about to happen. "What!" I ask. "I don't know Rick, I just feel it's going to be any moment now," says Bob. "Rick, isn't that a double wide mobile home on that trailer coming down the road on the other side?" asked Chrystal. "It is Hon, and looks like there's another trailer behind that one with the same load. Don't worry, Mary Jane's giving them plenty of room to get by," I said. "But babe, maybe I should call her and warn her about these crazy teenagers, I have her cell phone number," says Chrystal. "Don't let Chrystal do that Rick," Bob says in a firm tone.

"Whoa, why's that Bob?" I ask. "Have you forgotten the last time we got involved with changing somebody's destiny," replies Bob, "and that look the angel of death gave us. I never want to see that look again Rick, do you?" asked Bob. "No, I don't man," I replied. "Then, Rick, just pull over and let the whole thing unfold, and don't get involved." I tell Chrystal, "No, don't call Mary Jane, she knows what she's doing Hon, she's an old pro."

We were about to be passed by the first tractor trailer with the mobile home on it's back, just as I was backing off I looked over, and in that split second I see the little Honda car with all but one of the teenage girls screaming and throwing their arms about. The only one not screaming was the driver, because she was, believe it or not, "texting" a fucking message on her phone!

As I back way off it was like going backwards out of a tunnel. I look up to see the young fella driving the rig hauling that mobile home and catch the look on his face. This guy had nowhere to go because the road was built up with a three to four foot drop off to the desert for drainage on both sides. To make matters worst there's a big lavender Freightliner with it's forty foot trailer on his left. This young mans eyes were as big as silver dollars, as he brakes hard his load starts moving violently from side to side.

And like in a movie when they slow everything down at that critical moment when something's about to happen, that's what is happening right now in front of my eyes. As I back way off and watch, I look over and see the cute little blonde driving the lowered Honda. She finally looks up from her phone to see there's not enough room or time to do anything and starts to freak out. The red Toyota and green Pontiac had already backed way off and have pulled over behind me, thank God!

The fright on that girls face driving the Honda at that moment she realized she was fucked was like a scene out of a horror movie. I imagine that's the expression most people get on their face right at that moment when they think, ah shit, this is going to really hurt, and I hope I live through this.

She had no choice, but to try to get into in the spot that was only NOW available because I had backed way off. But, she was going way to fast to yank the steering wheel like that, and started to lose control right away. After all, she was probably only seventeen and had only been driving for a couple of weeks, if that?

I glance in my rear view mirror to see my friend Bob sitting up looking straight ahead with all the intensity of a cat stalking a mouse. Bobby suggests now is the time to pull over to the side of the road. Chrystal grabs her face in horror as the whole thing unfolds in front of us.

I've never felt so helpless, I thought. "I know Rick," Bobby says as he reads my thoughts. "Just stay in the car it will all be over soon," replies Bob. To the right we witness the Honda with the five girls inside go into a series of flips. It leaves a cloud of dust while barreling into the desert. Straight ahead of us Mary Jane is breaking so hard that her tractor is bouncing up and down violently and her trailer is swaying back and forth, but she's getting it under control. Wow, I think to myself what a good driver she is. "She sure is," says Bobby. And to my surprise it looks like the young man hauling the mobile home is also getting his rig under control.

～

As the dust settles in the desert we can see the Honda has come to a stop, and is on it's roof and Mary Jane has pulled to the side as far as she can.

Since we're now stopped ourselves, I ask Chrystal. "Call 911, tell them we are at mile marker 49 on Highway 95 heading north to Carson City." Chrystal shakes her head and starts to cry and says, "I'm glad Mary Jane is alright." "Me too babe," I reply.

Then I see it, the white Ford pick up seems to be coming straight towards us, and out of control, the two boys that were in the bed must have jumped out, when it turned around. In an instant, Bobby's inside the cab of the white Ford and pushes the driver out of the way, yanks the wheel to the right and slams on the brakes. The two boys in the Ford must have thought there was a ghost in the truck, man if they only knew, there was. The white Ford then comes screeching to a stop, just ahead of us and slowly drifts into the drainage ditch, just off the road in front of the rig hauling the first half of the Mobile home.

I look at my friend, who's now standing in front of our Buick starring at Chrystal and I, and shake my head in disbelief. "Thank you Bob, thank you man, how did you do that?" I ask him. Bobby gives me a very loving look, and simple nods, and says, "Your welcome."

I get out of the Buick and go over to the passenger side door next to Chrystal and look over to the Honda car again. I'm shocked and can't believe my eyes when I see Mary Jane and her husband, Joey, pulling those teenage girls from that smashed wreck laying on it's roof. "Bob, do you see that?" I ask. "I see it buddy," replies Bob. It takes me a moment and then it hits me like a ton of bricks, and I ask Bob, "Does this mean what I think it means, Bob?" "It does Rick, step over to the front of your car and look up the road," says Bob.

As I walk up to the front of my car and look up the road I see the driver of the mobile home hauler jump out of his rig and run over to Mary Jane's truck. The young boys from the Ford are now running up the road to her rig as well, and then I see her. "Oh no, Bob, tell me it's not so. Is Mary Jane, gone?" I ask.

"She is, Rick, after she pulled to the side she jumped out to see if she could help those girls, and just as she was stepping away from her rig it happened. The boys in the Ford had just turned around and were coming back, hauling ass trying get to their friends as quick as possible. They had just passed the second half of that mobile home and didn't see her step off her rig and onto the road in time. They were out of control, that's when they hit her." "She was killed instantly Rick." "Damn it Bob, I loved that lady," I said. "Amen to that my friend, I'm so sorry, she was a fine lady," said Bob. She and Joey are finally together again, I think to myself, as I watch them work as a team helping those new young souls. Joey, helping them out of the wreck and up to their feet, and Mary Jane greeting each one with a big hug.

"Honey, what's happening up the road, I want to see," says Chrystal as she gets out of the car. "You stay here babe, I'll go look first, please, stay, here," I say. As I already know what I'm about to see I go through the motions and make my way up to the lavender rig, there in the road is Mary Jane lying on her back just in front of her truck. Her head, laying in a small puddle of blood, her beautiful green eyes are still open. The other trucker is shaking while trying to cover her with a blanket. I grab him by the arm and still his hands and tell him to please wait, she was a friend of mine. As I kneel down to brush her silver hair off her forehead I can hear

Chrystal, standing right behind me, sobbing. With a broken heart my wife calls out her name "Mary Jane, please, God no." I reach back to pull Chrystal closer to me and use my other hand to close Mary Jane's eyes. Chrystal kneels down and softly grabs her hand and tells her goodbye. I look at my wife, smile and start to cry myself.

Bobby, who's now standing in the desert appears to be greeting Mary Jane. Mary Jane, hugs Bob and introduces him to Joey. "We've already met Sweetheart," he tells her. Then I hear Bob explain the whole story to her of how he went back to the jungle and found him. Mary Jane looked a little puzzled at first until he points over to me. He tells her about our current relationship and how we were buddies in life, and are even better friends now. As he explains about my gift, she looks me straight in the eyes and shakes her head. "You're a sly old fox now, aren't you sugar, what a wonderful gift that must be," says Mary Jane. "Does Chrystal know?" I just shake my head and tell her, "No." "Don't be sad for me darlin, I've been praying for this day for a long time now." She grabs her man's arm, they both look at each other and smile with such happiness, then look at me one last time and just say, "goodbye." I mouth the words "goodbye, Mom," she smiles again, and throws me a kiss. As I hear the sirens getting closer they both turn to Bob and say goodbye, and thank you Bobby. Bob replies, "you take care of that beautiful lady now Joey." Joey, just nods and salutes, and they slowly vanish from site.

As the first responders arrive they immediately drive their vehicle into the desert to the overturned Honda. The other trucker and the two young men from the white Ford have now gone over there as well to help pull the bodies out. One of the paramedics comes up to the road in time to witness my wife kiss our friend on the cheek then, cover Mary Jane's face with the blanket.

Bob, who's now back at my side and staring off into the desert turns and looks down at Mary Jane's body and says to me. "Rick, she must have touched a lot of lives both on and off the road, don't you think?" "I do buddy, she was a sweet gal," I reply. "Was, and still is," replies Bob. As I stand over my wife still kneeling over Mary Jane, I ask Bobby, "This didn't have to happen, did it?" "It did Rick," replies Bob, "It was her destiny." "Hey Bob, I wanted to thank you again, for what you did back there, you know, with the white Ford." "Your welcome, Rick, as much as I would have liked to have saved our new friend, I can only be at one place at a time and you and Chrystal mean the world to me." "Thanks brother."

Walking back to our car I couldn't help but notice something out of place. As I looked across the road at the front of the white Ford. There, stuck to the hood just above the grill, was Mary Jane's POW*MIA pin. I picked it off the hood and put it in my pocket.

CHAPTER 8.

Mom sure loved that song

When we get back home to our little town and pull into the parking lot of the old strip mall where the Moonglow is located I can't help but notice that it looks like a ghost town. Looking in the rear view mirror I was about to spout out some sort of stupid little ghost type joke to Bob, like hey Bob, there must be a meeting, didn't you get the memo, but decided not to. Then, just as quick as I changed my mind I remembered shit, he can read my thoughts, so I just looked in the mirror and smiled. Bobby raised his eyes from looking down and smiled back at me as if to say, it's alright, and then was gone.

Chrystal, and I step into the Moonglow to find it empty as well. Lenny is sitting at the end of the bar by the window watching a golf tournament on television. "Hey guys, how was your trip to Vegas?" he asked. Immediately Chrystal starts to softly cry and shake her head. "There was a terrible accident on the way back, Len," I replied. "Oh, what happened?" he asked. "I'll tell you later, buddy, but first I gotta ask, what's going on in town?" "It's the middle of the day, where is everybody?" I said. "Funeral for old man Rittenhouse is today," says Lenny. "I know he was pretty old, what happened?" I asked. "That was it," replied Lenny, "as far as I know he just died of old age." "Hmm, yeah, he had to be in his late eighty's, I think." "From what I heard he lied about his age for years, and was probably closer to ninety five say some of the older town folk that still come in for a quick pop," replied Lenny.

As Chrystal, comes out of the bathroom she asks Lenny for a 7up and I chime in with "and a Heineken for me please." "Well, that old boy sure did a lot for this town," I said. "No matter whether you liked him or not, if it weren't for him fighting the county fathers all those years to get things built, this town would still be the stage coach stop it was back in the gold rush days." "Is that right?" asked Lenny. "Tell me about the old boy." "Well, I didn't really know him very well, but I always thought he was a gentleman and a stand up guy," I replied. "I am pretty sure he was one of the richest people in this county, although you'd never know that if you didn't know him," I added. "Bob knew him real well, but then again Bob knew everybody."

"His wife must have been a real beauty when she was younger, don't you think?" asked Lenny. "Oh hell yeah," I said, "still is in my opinion. The way she dresses and wears her hair, and still sports a smoking hot body for an older gal, I think. Yeah, she's a very stunning lady."

"They've always been the friendliest of people, you could see it whenever they came to town, very much a part of the community… Her in that classic Jaguar," says Lenny. "Yeah, and him in his old red '56 Ford pickup," I replied. Hey, I wonder where Bob is? I thought to myself.

"You think he bought that truck brand new Rick?" asked Lenny. "I do, buddy," I replied. "I think he took care of everything he had, just look at the wife." "Hey, Lenny, did I ever tell you about that time when Bob and I were standing out in front of his shop and Mr. Rittenhouse got into it with that asshole environmentalist, Barry what's his name?" "No, but I know who you mean, that dude is just fucking creepy man. He came in here one time wearing a pair of cut off shorts so fucking short his boys were hanging out in the sunshine, one on either side, you know what I mean," says Lenny. "I do brother, yuk! Ah, shit, now I got that vision in my head." "So, then what happened?" I asked. "Well, I told him he would have to leave," said Lenny. "Really, and did he leave?" I asked. "Not before saying to me," "don't you know who I am?" "That did it for me, sent me over the freaking edge, you know what I mean? Cause then I had to tell him. Yeah, I know who you are, now you'll have to hurry the hell up and leave before I come over to your side of the bar, and show you just who I am. So anyway, go on with your story Rick, what happened?" Lenny replied. "Shit Len, that was a pretty good story right there, I loved it," I said.

"Well, I guess they were arguing over some fucking hiking trail the Barry guy wanted to put straight through Mr. Rittenhouse's property," I said. "What, you mean right through the mans property? You know, people in California got a lot of nerve, don't ya think Rick?" says Lenny. "Back in Colorado we don't tolerate that kinda shit, your land is your's, fence or no fence. It's a matter of respect," he adds.

"Here, in California, the birthplace of the Sierra Club and the ACLU, the land of fruits and nuts, as they say, they got a different way of looking at things," I replied. "Anyway, we heard all the yelling and looked over just in time to see Mr. R. take off his shoe and throw it at the jerk," I said. "His shoe, huh, what kind of shoe was it?" asked Lenny. "You know, I think was a white tennis shoe, a Reebok as a matter of fact." "Yeah, then what happened?" asked Lenny.

"Well, it was probably a good thing Mr. R. went over and picked up his shoe, cause right after he threw it the Barry guy threw his arms up and screamed like a little girl, then called 911 and threatened to sue. Funny how the Barry guy couldn't find a single witness when the Sherriff arrived. Busy day in town, too, people all over the place. I remember thinking that it was probably a good thing that it was 1996 and not 1896 because old Barry what's his name might have been laying face down in the dirt with a bullet in his chest," I said. "Sounds like Mr. R. was one good old boy Rick," says Lenny. "He was man," I replied, "he'll be missed."

"So, your trip?" asked Lenny. "Good, real good, thanks for asking Len," I replied. Then I look over to see Bob sitting on a bar stool just staring at me. "Hey dude, where you been?" I asked him. "Just saying goodbye to Mr. Rittenhouse, Rick. I saw him standing by the four way stop when we pulled into town and I just wanted to be the first to greet him and tell him farewell," says Bob. "So, is he still here, Bob?" "No, he's not. He was just passing through my realm, and I caught him before he moved on to the next, so to speak, and now he's gone for good."

"Hey Rick," says Bob, "there's something I've been wanting to ask you?" "Oh," I said, "what's that?" "I told you about what I saw on the back of your head some time ago and you haven't done anything about it yet, have you?" "Ah, no, not yet I haven't," I replied. "What's the matter with you, why aren't you taking this seriously?" asked Bob. "Do you want to be stuck over here in Spirit world with me? Or worse, don't make me go back east and tell your Mother."

"You wouldn't do that," I said. "Like hell, I won't. I will Rick, I'm not screwing around, so please, you have to take this seriously man," he replies.

"Wow, I think you really would, you asshole. So, since you put it that way I will, I promise," I said.

When we get home, I ask Chrystal to make me an appointment with Dr. Chen who's been our family doctor for thirty years. I tell her I've been having some headaches that just won't go away. "Oh, honey what do you think is wrong?" Chrystal asked. "Probably nothing sweetie, but at my age it's better to be safe than sorry, don't you think?" I said. "Hmm, you don't mind if I go along with you then, do you babe?" Chrystal replies.

Dr. Chen, is this cool little asian guy. I remember when we first met him I thought it was cool that this little five foot two asian fella drove a big 1975 red Cadillac El Dorado convertible. Hell, he could barley see over the steering wheel. Now here it is thirty years later and he drives a Prius, go figure? Anyway, as far as Chrystal's concerned he's saved my life more than once now. I guess we'd probably follow him anywhere, you know what they say, if you find a good barber or mechanic you stick with them. Same goes for a doctor in my opinion. I guess, I'm hoping he's got at least one more miracle in his bag of tricks for me.

After two weeks of driving to and from Sacramento for various tests, Mary his assistant calls us in for the results, which were not good. It seems I have a cancerous tumor at the base of my skull, and it is malignant, and I'll need surgery as soon as possible.

As Dr. Chen, was talking to me about the course of action I should take, my mind started wandering off.

I was keeping eye contact with him but was numb from what he just told me. As he spoke, it was like somebody turned down the volume, I wasn't hearing a word he said. I knew that my wife would fill me in on anything I missed when we got home, she always seems to hear stuff I missed. She can always tell when I zone off too, and now is one of those times. I guess like most people, I couldn't help but be sad, and think of how my life might be over soon. If I could have lived a better life, been a better husband, and father, you know, a better person. I thought, I sure hope I made the cut in God's eyes. I guess I might find out pretty soon though, huh?

I remember seeing Bobby, standing right behind the doctor saying something to me and Chrystal's mouth moving too, but I didn't hear any sound, from either of them. My mind, wandered back to the time when I was about six years old, riding a sled down that big hill near my childhood home in Baltimore. Then, I briefly closed my eyes while feeling the wind in my hair thinking, I was driving my jet boat across the lake, somewhere in my mid thirty's, and many thoughts in between. I thought, about a few of the things Chrystal and I did, you know the milestone's, having our one and only child Danielle, after Chrystal having several miscarriages, buying and fixing up our first home. All the fun and friends we've had through the years. But most of all, as I turn to look at her I think about how much this women has loved me. I remembered times when I was younger, working out of town during the week and coming home on the weekend. Thinking about her on my drive home always made me feel good, which always made me smile, and drive a little faster to get home to her. I thought too, about how she could have done so much better than me, I'm certainly a lucky man, that much I know.

I sure had some good times, I thought. I don't know how long I was in that daydream, but just as soon as Dr. Chen gave me a vitamin B12 shot I snapped right out of it. I looked over at my wife, and there was no explanation necessary, she knew I was somewhere else…Hmm, she knows me too well.

Because Chrystal and I trust Dr. Chen thoroughly, we let Mary in his office make all the arrangements. How long you been there Bob? I thought. "Long enough Rick, I hope you don't mind me popping in like this but I was worried about you man," said Bob. "It's not like I can just walk up to Crystal and ask her, now is it?" "No, I guess not pal, I'll bet she'd shit a gold brick if you did though."

"Well, good luck with the surgery my friend. I'll be right there with you in the operating room if you don't mind," says Bob. "No, of course I don't mind, I would actually like that a lot, just try not to get in the way," I said, with a wink. "Ha, I'll be sure not to do that," replies Bob, as he smiles, shakes his head then vanishes.

A couple of nights before the operation we had the kids over for dinner, Chrystal made a wonderful meal as always. I caught my daughter staring at me a few times, and each time I'd raise my eyebrows she would simply say "what?" which was her way of saying I love you Dad. My son in law, who's a real stand up kind guy, was reassuring me all night that everything was going to be alright; but just in case something does happen, not to worry. "Good to know," I told him.

My little one, as I like to call my nine year old granddaughter, was probably the most difficult of all because she stuck to me like a wet tee shirt all night. Every time she stared in my eyes, we both started to cry. As much as I tried to assure her that her 'Pop Pop' was going to be fine, there was that doubt that sort of hung in the room like an bad odor.

When the kids finally left after many hugs and kisses, Chrystal and I went to bed. As I went to turn the outside lights out I could see Bobby standing in the driveway, both hands in his pockets, giving me a nod and a wink. "I'll see you in the hospital pal," he said. "I know Buddy, thank you," I replied, "good night my friend."

"What are you looking at Babe?" Chrystal, asked me as she puts her arms around me. "Just the moon Hon," I say. "Ah Rick, the moon's at the back of the house," she says, and gives me that look.

∽

The day before the operation Chrystal and I just laid around the house and watched old movies and snuggled all day. There were a few phone calls from friends, but for the most part we let folks just leave a message. I only picked up the phone when it was family or a good pal was calling, all the others were, I think, just going through the motions. You know, like a stranger saying Merry Christmas. Anyway, as we sat on the sofa snuggling I told my lovely wife just how much she meant to me, I know she already knows that, but I think a women needs to hear that from time to time. When she told me she was really worried that something might happen I didn't know how to address that other than to just hold her in my arms and say nothing.

The next day we drove our '57 Buick to the hospital at 4 a.m. which was nice as there weren't many people on the road that early, so it was nice to put my foot in it again…Sweet.

After all the pre-op prep and introductions from the nurses and technicians who were going to be assisting the surgeon and anesthesiologist, I thought to myself, shit why do they do that? Chances are I may never meet them again but I guess it's like going to a concert where one musician will introduce all the other people on stage. I just smile, shake hands, say "hi" and leave it at that. Hell, I think I even met the hospital maintenance man and some guy delivering medical supplies. After all of that I felt tired so I dozed off for a nap.

They woke me just minutes before they were going to take me in to the O.R. I guess so I could say goodbye to my family, which I knew would be hard. So after many kisses and hugs again, it was time to get the show started. As they wheeled me down the hall I thought, how cool it was for them to wheel you in backwards so you can see your family one last time. As I wave to them all, I see my little one's bottom lip quivering as she tries to say, "Pop Pop, I love you," ahhh, "I love you too sweetheart," I told her. The sweet older nurse who's name tag reads Nora wipes my tears with a tissue. As they push the bed through the operating room doors she leans down and whispers to me, "calm down, your in good hands." She tells me to take a few calming deep breaths, which I do, then look up at her and smile.

In the operating room I see Bob, across the room, standing in the corner. "See you in a little while, Rick," he says. "Yeah, alright," and as quick as that I was out. I started to dream right away, and the dream I'm having is like nothing else I've ever had before, not that I can remember my dreams.

I can't and I think most people don't either, but sometimes after you wake up you do, even if just for a little while. And it's easier when it was a good dream. This, is one of those good dreams and the most realistic dream ever, if it is a dream at all.

The strangest part about this dream is first I get the most intense sensation all over my body as a warm rush from head to toe. So intense and so exhilarating that it actually hurt a little, but yet felt wonderful at the same time. Then, I feel a new warmth come over me, along with a light breeze, and then I hear very relaxing music. I'm fighting to open my eyes, because I'm not sure if I'm dreaming or still on the operating table or what.

I finally give in and I open my eyes I get the answer to my question. I'm still on the operating table but I'm also standing on the other side of the room looking at myself, lying there. WTH, I think, then I hear, "Hey Buddy." I turn my head and see my buddy Bob standing there and say, "Oh no, Bobby, please tell me this is a dream." "I wish I could Rick, but it's not a dream, you died." I turn back to see the doctors and nurses trying everything in their power, scrambling to save me. I watched them work on me feverishly and nothing seemed to help, so, they finally had to give up. Sadness fills the room like a dark cloud. The OR doctor and his staff, seemed to all pause for a moment, and I could see the sadness written all over their faces as they, one, by one left the room. Bobby, puts his arm around my shoulder and says, "I'm sorry my friend."

I want to cry but I can't. Bob, says there's no need for tears in this place, and not to worry, he'll show me how to cope here. Nora, the nurse who wiped my eyes earlier brings Chrystal into the room, and as the door swings shut I can see my family down the hall with stunned faces. My little one is crying hysterically and screaming for her Pop Pop, my daughter holding her in her arms.

"Damn, Bob, this is hard to watch. Do I have to stay here?" "No Rick, you can leave whenever you like, where would you rather be?" "Anywhere Buddy, just take me away from here." As we start to walk away a long white corridor appears on the back wall, it appears to be endless.

Bob, with his arm still around my shoulder leads me towards it. As I enter the corridor I look back one last time at the love of my life, and see Chrystal standing by my head on the operating table. She has her hands on either side of my face, her tears looked like a soft rain falling on my face. Her eyes are closed and she's praying to Jesus with all her heart to bring her man back to her. "Please Lord, bring my Ricky back to me," I hear her say… and it's tearing my heart out.

"Take me away from here Bob," and just like that we were in a place that looked like a big empty warehouse; the walls, ceiling and floor, all white. Bob, and I are shades of black and gray, and soon landscape and trees appear but in shades of black and gray as well. "Is this the way it is Bob, void of all color?" "Yeah, that's the way it is here, Rick, although I think it must get nicer each time you move on." "Really?" "Well, I'm not sure, but I hope it does pal, didn't it say somewhere in the good book 'My fathers mansion has many rooms.' Anyway, that's my hope." Said Bob.

"How many dimensions or rooms are there, Bob?" "My best guess would have to be many Rick, most of them, thank God go the same direction we're going," replied Bob. "But some do go the other way?" I asked. "Yeah, but you don't have to worry about that buddy. Although you might hear an occasional scream of pain from some poor bastard as they go zipping right through here on their way toward hell." "Train don't stop here, huh Bob?" "Nope, never does pal." "Anyway Rick, I'm sorry you're here my friend. I'll show you everything I know, and then you'll be on your own, okay? That's the way it works here." "Will I still see you?" "As long as I'm here you will, or until one of us moves on. But for now, what can I show you?" "Take me back to the east coast, my friend." "Good call Rick, just think about it with all your heart and you'll be there."

The next thing I knew I was standing on the sidewalk in front of my sister Linda's house in Baltimore. As I make my way up the walkway, I see the very faint figure of my Mother coming through the front door with her arms open wide to greet me. As I climb the steps she's waiting for me on the porch. She's smiling at me and also, crying, and I ask her, "Mom, can you see me?" Just as I reach the top of the stairs my Mother reaches for me and pulls me into her arms, to embrace me. Her touch was just as I remembered, so soft and delicate, like satin. Boy, how I missed her.

I couldn't help but squeeze her in my arms like I'd never done before. I caught myself and thought, I better not squeeze to hard, I may hurt my Mom. And like Bobby, Mom could also read my thoughts, and told me, "Not to worry Ricky, you go ahead and squeeze me as hard as you like. I missed you too, son." Bob had told me earlier that this realm is void of scent, but I don't believe that. Holding my Mom I'm sure I can smell her perfume, and the flood of emotions almost knocked me over. "Mom, there's so much I want to tell you." "I know son, I've been watching all my children since I've passed on."

"Mom, I'm sorry I wasn't there when you passed, I"... "You were there son, when your brother Jon, held the phone to my ear in the hospital, I heard every word you said. I could not have been more proud of you, you've always been there in my heart, Ricky, as are all my children." "Now I want you to go home, you don't belong here." "But how do I do that, Mom? I died on the operating table, and can never go back." "Oh, but your wrong son, you've been given a special gift and along with your good mate, Bob, you'll help many more people find their way as they cross over. I want you to go back now, and promise me you'll take care of those girls of yours." "Alright Mom, but how do I get back?" "Bobby, be a good lad and please take my boy back to his girls, will you dear?" "Yes, of course Ms. Vera," replies Bob. "I love you, Mom." "I know son," my mom says, as she leans forward and kisses me on the cheek and whispers, "goodbye for now, love." "Goodbye Mum."

"Bob, before we go I'd like to go by the old house to see"… "I know pal, you want to see if your brother is there." "Yeah, I do, you don't mind do you?" I ask. "Course not," answers Bob.

As we walk up the sidewalk to Mom's old house, Tony is sitting on the porch glider still looking as sad as before. "Tony, it's me, Rick." "Rick, what are you doing here?" "It's a long story Tony, I came by to tell you that you have to leave this place. Mom will never be here again, and you need to start on your journey." "What?" "Just come with me for a short walk and someone will meet us down the road to guide you." "Okay, I guess," Tony says. I don't know how I knew that, but I did. Sure enough, as we started walking down the street in this black and white realm a dark shadowy, very unimposing figure appeared and took my brother by the hand and then vanished in just a few steps. "Who was that, Bob?" "I don't know Rick, but we don't want to follow them, that I do know." " Are you ready to go back home now?" "I am buddy, let's go." "Okay, now, just close your eyes and click your heals together three times." "Say what, are you shitting me, Bob?" "Of course I am, gotcha, good huh, Rick?"

And just as quick as I thought of my wife standing over me, I was there, back in the operating room standing in the corner with Bobby. Chrystal, was all alone in the room with me now, her head on my chest, softly crying and humming an old Johnny Mathis tune that my Mother used to love. "Well, what do I do now Bob?" "Hell if I know dude, I guess we wait." "Hey, Bob, I want to thank you man." As I can only now, grab my buddy and give him a hug, I take this opportunity, to do just that. "Really, Bob, thank you man for all you've done for me." "I don't know if I've ever told you this, but I want you to know that I love you like a brother buddy." "I feel the same way pal, and after you get better, I'll be by to see you 'cause we gotta talk about this gift your Mom mentioned." Bob said. "Okay dude," I reply. "And remember Rick, 'our feet are the same'." "Ha, I see you speak the Swedish, huh Bob? I'll see you later too, pal."

Nora, the O.R head nurse steps into the room and comes over to my wife. She puts her hand on Chrystal's arm and says, "If you need more time we'd like to move your husband into a private room so the family can say their goodbye's." Chrystal raises her head off my chest still holding my hand, nods and replies, "Yes, thank you, that would be nice."

And just as before when I passed over I get a rush from head to toe, only this time it's cold, like stepping outside to get the paper in the winter, wearing just your underwear cold, damn. All of sudden I'm hearing Chrystal's voice on my chest and she's still deep in prayer. "Dear Lord, please, please, bring my Ricky back to me"…I open my eyes and find Chrystal's hands. I take hold of one and lightly squeeze it, then start to quietly sing. "And I say to myself it's wonderful, wonderful, oh so wonderful, my love."

With the warmest, most beautiful blue eyes on the planet my lady looks down at me, and says, "There's my man, thank you God." "How long was I gone Hon?" I asked her. "Nearly 10 minutes, sweetheart," she says. "Honey, why were you humming that Johnny Mathis tune?" I asked.

"I don't know babe, while I was in prayer, I also turned to your Mother, and I asked her to please ask God, to send you back to me, and that song just popped into my head." "I guess, because I knew how much she loved that song, she sent it to me. When I started to hum the tune I felt the warmth from your chest on my face, and then I just knew everything was going to be alright," Chrystal whispered to me. "Yeah, Mom, sure loved that song, huh babe?"

The End.

My buddy Bob Moore

My wife Christy [Chrystal] and me

Jim Lillpop [Lenny]

Ryan [son in law] Danielle, Amie, Me & Christy

My Mom 'Vera May Blanchard'

Brother Tony, Mom and brother Jon…RIP

Rick Nicholson was a building contractor for over thirty years. Now retired, he currently lives in the Sierra foothills of Northern California with his wife, Christy; their daughter, Danielle; her husband, Ryan; and their daughter, Amie. Rick enjoys a fine bottle of wine and a good cigar with family and friends accompanied by much laughter and good stories.